Christine Rimmer came to her profession the long way around. She tried everything from acting to teaching to telephone sales. Now she's finally found work that suits her perfectly. She insists she never had a problem keeping a job—she was merely gaining "life experience" for her future as a novelist. Christine lives with her family in Oregon. Visit her at christinerimmer.com.

Same Time, Next Christmas

CHRISTINE RIMMER

MILLS & BOON

First published in Great Britain 2018
by Mills & Boon, an imprint of HarperCollins*Publishers*
1 London Bridge Street, London, SE1 9GF

Large Print edition 2019

© 2018 Christine Rimmer

ISBN: 978-0-263-08332-3

MIX
Paper from
responsible sources
FSC   FSC® C007454
www.fsc.org

This book is produced from independently certified
FSC™ paper to ensure responsible forest management.
For more information visit www.harpercollins.co.uk/green.

Printed and bound in Great Britain
by CPI Group (UK) Ltd, Croydon, CR0 4YY

For MSR, always.

Chapter One

December 23, four years ago...

Even with the rain coming down so hard he could barely make out the twisting gravel road ahead of him, Matthias Bravo spotted the light shining through the trees.

The Jeep lurched around another twist in the road. For a few seconds before the trees obscured his view, Matt could see his getaway cabin in the clearing up ahead. Yep. The light was coming from the two windows that flanked the front door.

Some idiot had broken in.

Swearing under his breath, Matt steered his Jeep to the almost nonexistent side of the road and switched off the engine and lights.

The rain poured down harder, pounding the roof, roaring so loud he couldn't hear himself think. Out the windshield, the trees with their moss-covered trunks were a blur through the rippling curtain made of water.

Should he have just stayed home in Valentine Bay for Christmas?

Probably. His injured leg throbbed and he was increasingly certain he'd caught that weird bug his brothers had warned him about. He had a mother of a headache and even though he'd turned the heater off several miles back, he was sweating.

"Buck up, buddy." He slapped his own cheek

just to remind himself that torrential rain, a sliced-up leg, a headache and a fever were not the worst things he'd ever lived through.

And at the moment, he had a mission. The SOB in his cabin needed taking down—or at the very least, roughing up a tad and kicking out on his ass.

Matt kept his rifle in a hidden safe at the back of the Jeep. Unfortunately, the safe was accessed through the rear door.

"No time like the present to do what needs doing."

Yeah. He was talking to himself. Kind of a bad sign.

Was he having a resurgence of the PTSD he'd been managing so well for over a year now?

No. Uh-uh. Zero symptoms of a recurrence. No more guilt than usual. He wasn't drunk and hadn't been in a long time. No sleep problems, depression or increased anxiety.

Simply a break-in he needed to handle.

And going in without a weapon? How stupid would that be?

He put on his field jacket, pulled up the hood, shoved open his door and jumped out, biting back a groan when his hurt leg took his weight.

The good news: it wasn't that far to the rear door. In no time, he was back inside the vehicle, sweating profusely, dripping rain all over the seat, with the rifle in one hand and a box of shells in the other.

Two minutes later, rifle loaded and ready for action, he was limping through the downpour toward the cabin. Keeping to the cover of the trees, he worked his way around the clearing, doing a full three-sixty, checking for vehicles and anyone lurking outside, finding nothing that shouldn't be there.

Recon accomplished, he approached the building from the side. Dropping to the wet ground, he crawled to the steps, staying low as he climbed them. His leg hurt like hell, shards of pain stabbing him with every move he made. It was bleeding again right through the thick makeshift bandage he'd tied on the wound.

Too bad. For now, he needed to block the pain and focus.

As he rolled up onto the covered porch, he swiped back his dripping hood and crawled over beneath the front window.

With slow care, he eased up just enough to peer over the sill.

He got an eyeful.

A good-looking brunette—midtwenties, he would guess—sat on the hearth, warming herself at a blazing fire. She wore only a bra and panties. Articles of clothing lay spread out around her, steaming as they dried.

Was she alone? He didn't see anyone else in there. The cabin was essentially one big room, with bath and sleeping loft. From his crouch at the window, he could see the bathroom, its door wide open. Nobody in there. And he had a straight visual shot right through to the back door. Nada. Just the pretty, half-naked brunette.

She looked totally harmless.

Still, he should check the situation out from every possible angle before making his move.

Was he maybe being a little bit paranoid? Yeah, possibly.

But better safe than sorry.

He dragged himself over beneath the other front window. The view from there was pretty much the same. The woman looked so innocent, leaning back on her hands now, long, smooth legs stretched out and crossed at the ankles. She raised a slim hand and forked her fingers through her thick, dark hair.

Grimly, he pulled up his hood and crawled down the steps into the deluge again. Circling the cabin once more, close-in this time, he ducked to peer into each window as he passed.

Every view revealed the leggy brunette, alone, drying off by the fire.

By the time he limped back to the front of the building and crept up onto the porch again, he was all but certain the woman was on her own.

Still, she could be dangerous. Maybe. And dangerous or not, she *had* broken in and helped herself to his firewood. Not to mention he still couldn't completely discount the possibility that there was someone upstairs.

He'd just have to get the jump on her, hope

she really was alone and that no damn fool hid in the loft, ready to make trouble.

Sliding to the side, Matt came upright flush against the front door. Slowly and silently, he turned the knob. The knob had no lock, but he needed to see if the dead bolt was still engaged. It was. He took the keys from his pocket. At the speed of a lazy snail, in order not to alert the trespasser within, he unlocked the dead bolt.

That accomplished, he put the keys away and turned the knob with agonizing slowness until the door was open barely a crack. Stepping back, he kicked the door wide. It slammed against the inside wall as he leveled the barrel of his rifle on the saucer-eyed girl.

"Freeze!" he shouted. "Do it now!"

Sabra Bond gaped at the armed man who filled the wide-open doorway.

He was a very big guy, dressed for action in camo pants, heavy boots and a hooded canvas coat. And she wore nothing but old cotton panties and a sports bra.

No doubt about it. Her life was a mess—and getting worse by the second.

Sheepishly, she put her hands up.

The man glared down the barrel of that rifle at her. "What do you think you're doing in my cabin?"

"I, um, I was on my way back to Portland from my father's farm," she babbled. "I parked at the fish hatchery and started hiking along the creek toward the falls. The rain came. It got so bad that I—"

"Stop." He swung the business end of his rifle upward toward the loft. "Anyone upstairs? Do not lie to me."

"No one." He leveled the weapon on her again. "Just me!" she squeaked. "I swear it."

She waited for him to lower the gun. No such luck. The barrel remained pointed right at her. And, for some incomprehensible reason, she couldn't quit explaining herself. "I was hiking and thinking, you know? The time got away from me. I'd gone miles before the rain started. It kept getting worse, which led me to the unpleasant discovery that my waterproof jacket is only water resistant. Then I found your cabin…"

"And you broke in," he snarled.

Had she ever felt more naked? Highly unlikely. "I was just going to stand on the porch and wait for the rain to stop. But it only came down harder and I kept getting colder."

"So you broke in," he accused again, one side of his full mouth curling in a sneer.

Okay, he had a point. She *had* broken in. "I jimmied a window and climbed through," she admitted with a heavy sigh.

Still drawing a bead on her, water dripping from his coat, he stepped beyond the threshold and kicked the door shut. Then he pointed the gun at her pack. "Empty that. Just turn it over and dump everything out."

Eager to prove how totally unthreatening she was, Sabra grabbed the pack, unzipped it, took it by the bottom seam and gave it a good shake. A first-aid kit, an empty water bottle, a UC Santa Cruz Slugs hat and sweatshirt, and a bottle of sunscreen dropped out.

"Pockets and compartments, too," he commanded.

She unhooked the front flap and shook it some more. Her phone, a tube of lip balm, a comb and a couple of hair elastics tumbled to the floor. "That's it." She dropped the empty pack. "That's all of it." When he continued to glare at her, she added, "Dude. It was only a day hike."

"No gun." He paced from one side of the cabin to the other. She realized he was scoping out the upstairs, getting a good look at whatever might be up there.

Apparently satisfied at last that she really was alone, he pointed the gun her way all over again and squinted at her as though trying to peer into her brain and see what mayhem she might be contemplating.

Hands still raised, she shook her head. "I'm alone. No gun, no knives, no nothing. Just me in my underwear and a bunch of soggy clothes—and listen. I'm sorry I broke in. It was a bad choice on my part." *And not the only one I've made lately.* "How 'bout if I just get dressed and go?"

He studied her some more, all squinty-eyed and suspicious. Then, at last, he seemed to accept the fact that she was harmless. He lowered the rifle. "Sorry," he grumbled. "I'm overcautious sometimes."

"Apology accepted," she replied without a single trace of the anger and outrage the big man deserved—because no longer having to stare down the dark barrel of that gun?

Just about the greatest thing that had ever happened to her.

As she experienced the beautiful sensation of pure relief, he emptied the shells from his rifle, stuffed them in a pocket and turned to hang the weapon on the rack above the door. The moment he turned his back to her, she grabbed her Slugs sweatshirt and yanked it on over her head.

When he faced her again, he demanded, "You got anyone you can call to come get you?" She was flipping her still-damp hair out from under the neck of the sweatshirt as he added, "Someone with four-wheel drive.

They'll probably need chains or snow tires, too." When she just stared in disbelief, he said, "That frog strangler out there? Supposed to turn to snow. Soon."

A snowstorm? Seriously? "It is?"

He gave a snort of pure derision. "Oughtta check the weather report before you go wandering off into the woods."

Okay, not cool. First, he points a gun at her and then he insults her common sense. The guy was really beginning to annoy her. Sabra had lived not fifteen miles from this cabin of his for most of her life. Sometimes you couldn't count on the weather report and he ought to know that. "I did check the weather. This morning, before I left on my way to Portland. Light rain possible, it said."

"It's Oregon. The weather can change."

His condescending response didn't call for an answer, so she didn't give him one. Instead, she grabbed her still-soggy pants and put them on, too, wishing she'd had sense enough to keep driving right past the sign for the fish hatchery. A hike along the creek to the falls had seemed like a good idea at the time, a way to lift her spirits a little, to clear her troubled mind before going on back to Portland to face finding a new apartment during the remaining two weeks and two days of her vacation from work—a vacation that was supposed to have been her honeymoon.

The big guy grunted. "And you didn't answer my question. Got anyone you can call?"

"Well, let me see…" Her mom had been dead for six years now. Her dad was three hours away in Eugene until New Year's. Five days ago, on the day before she was supposed to have gotten married, she and her ex-fiancé had called it quits for reasons too upsetting to even think about at the moment. And she just wasn't ready to ask any of her Portland friends to drive eighty miles through a blizzard on the day before Christmas Eve to save her from a stranger with a bad attitude in an isolated cabin in the middle of the forest. "No. I don't have anyone to call."

The big guy did some swearing. Finally, he muttered, "Let me get my tree in here and I'll drive you wherever you need to go."

Get outta town. Mr. Grouchy Pants had a *tree*? She was almost as surprised as when he'd kicked open the door. "Uh, you mean *you* have a Christmas tree?"

His scowl deepened. "It's Christmas, isn't it?"

She put up both hands again. "It's just, well, you don't seem like the Christmas-tree type."

"I like Christmas." He narrowed his blue eyes at her. "I like it *alone*."

"Gotcha. And thank you—for the offer of

a ride, I mean. If you can get me to my car at the fish hatchery, I can take it from there just fine. As for the tree, I'll help you bring it in."

"You stay here. I don't need you."

"Good to know." She tugged on her socks and boots and not-quite-waterproof jacket as he pulled a tree stand out from under the sink, filled it with water and put it down near the door—and now that she wasn't terrified half out of her wits, she noticed that he was limping.

His right pants leg was torn up, hanging in tatters to the knee. Beneath the tatters, she could see a bit of bloody bandage—a very bloody bandage, actually, bright red and wet. It looked like he was bleeding into his boot.

He straightened from positioning the tree stand and took the three steps to the door.

She got up. "Do you know that you're bleeding?" He didn't bother to answer. She followed him outside. "Listen. Slow down. Let me help you."

"Stay on the porch." He growled the command as he flipped up the hood of his jacket and stepped out into the driving rain again. "I'll bring my Jeep to the steps."

She waited—because, hey. If he didn't want her help, he wasn't going to get it. Still, she felt marginally guilty for just standing there with a porch roof over her head as she watched him limp off into the downpour.

He vanished around the first turn in the road. It was getting dark. She wrapped her arms across her middle and refused to worry about that bloody bandage on his leg and the way he walked with a limp—not to mention he'd looked kind of flushed, hadn't he? Like maybe he had a fever in addition to whatever was going on with that leg...

Faintly, she heard a vehicle start up. A moment later, a camo-green Jeep Rubicon rolled into sight. It eased to a stop a few feet from the steps and the big guy got out. She pulled up her hood and ran down to join him as he began untying the tree lashed to the rack on the roof.

He didn't argue when she took the top end. "I'll lead," was all he said.

Oh, no kidding—and not only because he was so damn bossy. It was a thick noble fir with a wide circle of bottom branches that wouldn't make it through the door any other way.

He assumed the forward position and she trotted after him, back up the steps and into the warmth of the cabin. At the tree stand, he got hold of the trunk in the middle, raising it to an upright position.

She crouched down to guide it into place and tighten the screws, sitting back on her heels when the job was done. "Okay. You can let it go." He eyed her warily from above, his giant arm engulfed by the thick branches as he gripped the trunk. His face was still flushed and there were beads of moisture at his hairline—sweat, not rain, she would take a bet on that. "It's in and it's stable, I promise you," she said.

With a shrug, he let go.

The tree stood tall. It was glorious, blue-green and well shaped, the branches emerging in perfectly balanced tiers, just right for displaying strings of lights and a treasure trove of ornaments. Best of all, it smelled of her sweetest memories, of Christmases past, when her mom was still alive. Ruth Bond had loved Christmas. Every December, she would fill their house at Berry Bog Farm with all the best Christmas smells—evergreen, peppermint, cinnamon, vanilla…

"Not bad," he muttered.

She put away her memories. They only made her sad, anyway. "It's a beauty, all right."

He aimed another scowl at her. "Good, then. Get your gear and let's go." Was he swaying on his feet?

She rose to her height. "I don't know what's wrong with your leg, but you don't look well. You'd better sit down and let me see what I can do for you."

"I'm fine."

"Get real. You are not fine and you are getting worse."

He only grew more mulish. "We're leaving."

"I'm not getting in that Jeep with you behind the wheel." She braced her hands on her hips. He just went on glaring, swaying gently on his feet like a giant tree in a high wind. She quelled her aggravation at his pigheadedness and got busy convincing him he should trust her to handle whatever was wrong with him. "I was raised on a farm not far from here. My mom was a nurse. She taught me how to treat any number of nasty injuries. Just let me take a look at your leg."

"I'll deal with that later."

"You are wobbling on your feet and your face is red. You're sweating. I believe you have a fever."

"Did I ask for your opinion?"

"It's not safe for you to be—"

"I'm fine."

"You're not."

"Just get your stuff, okay?"

"No. Not okay." She made a show of taking off her jacket and hanging it by the door. "I'm not leaving this cabin until we've dealt with whatever's going on with your leg."

There was a long string of silent seconds— a battle of wills. He swayed and scowled. She did nothing except stand there and wait for the big lug to give in and be reasonable.

In the end, reason won. "All right," he said. He shrugged out of his coat and hung it up next to hers. And then, at last, he limped to the Navajo-print sofa in the center of the room and sat down. He bent to his injured leg—and paused to glance up at her. "When I take off this dressing, it's probably going to be messy. We'll need towels. There's a stack of old ones in the bathroom, upper left in the wooden cabinet."

She went in there and got them.

When she handed them over, he said, "And a first-aid backpack, same cabinet, lower right." He set the stack of towels on the sofa beside him.

"I've got a first-aid kit." It was still on the floor by the hearth where she'd dumped it when he'd ordered her to shake out her pack. She started for it.

"I saw your kit," he said. She paused to glance back at him as he bent to rip his pants leg wider, revealing an impressively muscular, bloodstained, hairy leg. "Mine's bigger."

She almost laughed as she turned for the bathroom again. "Well, of course it is."

His kit had everything in it but an operating table.

She brought it into the main room and set it down on the plank floor at the end of the sofa. He'd already pushed the pine coffee table to the side, spread towels on the floor in front of him and rolled his tattered pants leg to midthigh, tying the torn ends together to keep them out of the way.

She watched as he unlaced his boot. A bead of sweat dripped down his face and plopped to his thigh. "Here." She knelt. "I'll ease it off for you."

"I've got it." With a grunt, he removed the

boot. A few drops of blood fell to the towels. His sock was soggy with it, the blood soaking into the terrycloth when he put his foot back down.

"Interesting field dressing." She indicated the article of clothing tied around his lower leg.

One thick shoulder lifted in a half shrug. "Another T-shirt bites the dust."

"Is it stuck to the wound?"

"Naw. Wound's too wet." He untied the knots that held the T-shirt in place.

When he took the bloody rag away, she got a good look at the job ahead of her. The wound was an eight-inch crescent-shaped gash on the outside of his calf. It was deep. With the makeshift bandage gone, the flap of sliced flesh flopped down. At least it didn't appear to go all the way through to the bone. Blood dripped from it sluggishly.

"Let me see…" Cautiously, so as not to

spook him, she placed her index and middle fingers on his knee and gave a gentle push. He accepted her guidance, dipping the knee inward so she could get a closer look at the injury. "Butterfly bandages won't hold that together," she said. "Neither will glue. It's going to need stitches."

For the first time since he'd kicked open the door, one side of his mouth hitched up in a hint of a smile. "I had a feeling you were going to say that." His blue eyes held hers. "You sure you're up for this?"

"Absolutely."

"You really know what to do?"

"Yes. I've sewn up a number of injured farm animals and once my dad got gored by a mean bull when my mom wasn't home. I stitched him right up."

He studied her face for a good five seconds. Then he offered a hand. "Matthias Bravo."

She took it. "Sabra Bond."

Chapter Two

Sabra washed up at the kitchen-area sink, turning and leaning against the counter as she dried her hands. "Got a plastic tub?"

"Under the sink." He seemed so calm now, so accepting. "Look. I'm sorry if I scared you, okay?" His eyes were different, kinder.

She nodded. "I broke in."

"I overreacted."

She gazed at him steadily. "We're good."

A slow breath escaped him. "Thanks."

For an odd, extended moment, they simply stared at each other. "Okay, then," she said finally. "Let's get this over with."

Grabbing the tub from under the sink, she filled it with warm water and carried it over to him. As he washed his blood-caked foot and lower leg, she laid out the tools and supplies she would need. His first-aid pack really did have everything, including injectable lidocaine.

"Lucky man," she said. "You get to be numb for this."

"Life is good," he answered lazily, leaning against the cushions, letting his big head fall back and staring kind of vacantly at the crisscrossing beams overhead.

Wearing nitrile gloves from his fancy kit, she mopped up blood from around the injury and then injected the painkiller. Next, she irrigated the wound just the way her mom had taught her to do.

As she worked, he took his own temperature. "Hundred and two," he muttered unhappily.

She tipped her head at the acetaminophen and the tall glass of water she'd set out for him. "Take the pills and drink the water."

He obeyed. When he set the empty glass back down, he admitted, "This bug's been going around. Two of my brothers had it. Laid them out pretty good. At least it didn't last long. I was feeling punk this morning. I told myself it was nothing to worry about…"

"Focus on the good news," she advised.

"Right." He gave her a wry look. "I'm sick, but if I'm lucky, I won't be sick for long."

She carried the tub to the bathroom, dumped it, rinsed it and left it there. When she returned to him, she repositioned the coffee table, sat on the end of it and covered her thighs with a towel. "Let's see that leg." She tapped her knees with her palms, and he stretched the injured leg across them.

"Can you turn your leg so the wound is up and keep it in that position?"

"No problem." He rolled his foot inward, turning his outer calf up.

She put on a fresh pair of gloves and got to work.

It took a lot of stitches to do the job. He seemed content to just sprawl there, staring at the ceiling as she sewed him up.

But, now she had him at her mercy, there were a few questions she wanted to ask. "Did somebody come after you with an ax?" He lifted his head and mustered a steely stare. She grinned in response. It was so strange. Not long ago, he'd scared the crap out of her. Yet now he didn't frighten her in the least. She actually felt completely comfortable kidding him a little. "Do not make me hurt you."

He snorted. "It's embarrassing."

"I'll never tell a soul."

"It was raining when I cut down that tree. I forgot to bring gloves and my hands were soaking wet. Plus, I was feeling pretty bad from this damn bug I seem to have caught."

She tied off a stitch. "So then, what you're telling me is you almost chopped off your own leg?"

He let his head fall back again. "I come from a long line of woodsmen on my mother's side," he said wearily. "No self-respecting member of my family ever got hurt while cutting down an eight-foot tree."

"Until you."

"Go ahead, Sabra Bond, rub it in."

"Where'd you get that tree?" She tied off

another stitch. "I didn't see a tag on it. Have you been poaching, Matthias?"

"You can call me Matt." He said it in a lovely, low rumble that made her think of a purring cat—a very large one. The kind that could easily turn dangerous. "Everyone calls me Matt."

"I kind of like Matthias."

"Suit yourself."

"I'll ask again. Did you steal that gorgeous tree from the people of Oregon?"

He grunted. "I'll have you know I'm a game warden, a Fish and Wildlife state trooper. I *catch* the poachers—so no, I didn't steal that tree. I took it from property that belongs to my family."

"Ah. All right, then. I guess I won't have to turn you in."

"You can't imagine my relief."

"I have another question."

"Why am I not surprised?"

"Didn't it occur to you to head for a hospital or an urgent care after you took that ax to your leg?"

He didn't answer immediately. She was considering how much to goad him when he muttered, "Pride and denial are powerful things."

By the time she'd smoothed antibiotic ointment over the stitched-up wound and covered it with a bandage, he was sweating more heavily than ever. She helped him off with his other boot. "Come on," she coaxed. "Stretch out on the sofa, why don't you?"

"Just for a few minutes," he mumbled, but remained sitting up. He started emptying his pockets, dragging out his phone, keys and wallet, dropping them next to the lamp on the little table at the end of the sofa. From another pocket, he took the shells from his rifle.

He put them on the little table, too, and then leaned back against the cushions again.

She asked, "Do you have another sock to keep that bare foot warm?"

"You don't have to—"

"Just tell me where it is."

He swiped sweat from his brow. "In the dresser upstairs, top drawer, left."

Sabra ran up there and came down with a pillow from the bed and a clean pair of socks. She propped the pillow against one arm of the sofa and knelt to put on the socks for him. By then, he wasn't even bothering to argue that she didn't need to help him. He looked exhausted, his skin a little gray beneath the flush of fever.

She plumped the pillow she'd taken from the bed upstairs. "Lie down, Matthias." He gave in and stretched out, so tall that his feet hung off the end. "Here you go." She settled an afghan over him and tucked it in around him. "Okay, I'll be right back." And she hustled over to the sink to run cold water on a cloth.

"Feels good," he said, when she gently rubbed the wet cloth across his forehead and over his cheeks. "So nice and cool. Thank you…" Under the blanket, his injured leg jerked. He winced and stifled a groan. The lidocaine was probably wearing off. But the acetaminophen should be cutting the pain a little—and lowering his fever.

"Just rest," she said softly.

"All right. For few minutes, maybe. Not long. I'll be fine and I'll take you where you need to go."

She made a sound of agreement low in her throat, though she knew he wasn't going anywhere for at least a day or two.

Within ten minutes, he was asleep.

Quietly, so as not to wake him, she cleaned

up after the impromptu medical procedure. She even rinsed out his bloody boot and put it near the hearth to dry.

Two hours later, at a little after eight in the evening, Matthias was still on the couch. He kept fading in and out of a fevered sleep. There wasn't much Sabra could do for him but bathe his sweaty face to cool him off a little and retuck the blanket around him whenever he kicked it off.

She put another log on the fire and went through the cupboards and the small fridge in the kitchen area. He had plenty of food, the nonperishable kind. Beans. Rice. Flour. Pasta. Cans of condensed milk, of vegetables and fruit. She opened some chili and ate it straight from the can, washing it down with a glass of cold water.

Matthias slept on, stirring fitfully, muttering to himself. Now and then he called out the names of men, "Mark, no!" and "Nelson, don't do it!" and "Finn, where are you?" as if in warning or despair. He also muttered a woman's name, "Christy," more than once and vowed in a low, ragged rumble, "Never again."

He woke around nine. "Sabra?" he asked, his voice dry. Hoarse.

"Right here."

"Water?"

She brought him a tall glassful. "Don't get up. Let me help." She slipped her free hand under his big, sweaty head and held the glass to his mouth as he drained it.

With a whispered "Thank you" and a weary sigh, he settled against the pillow again.

She moistened another cloth in the icy water from the sink and bathed his face for him. "You know what, Matthias?"

"Ungh?"

"I'm going to go ahead and unload your Jeep for you."

He made another low sound in his throat. She decided to take that sound for agreement.

"Well, great." She patted his shoulder. "I'll just get after that, then. Go back to sleep." Scooping his keys off the side table, she put on her jacket and quietly tiptoed out to the porch.

The gorgeous sight that greeted her stole her breath and stopped her in her tracks.

Just as Matthias had predicted, the rain had turned to snow. She gazed at a world gone glittering white.

In the golden light that spilled out the cabin windows, the fat flakes fell thick and heavy. They'd piled up on the ground and decorated the branches of the western hemlock and Sitka spruce trees. There was a good three inches already.

"So beautiful," she whispered aloud and all

of her worries just fell away, both at the mess that currently added up to her life and the challenges she'd faced in the past few hours.

How could she be anything but happy in this moment? Christmas was falling from the sky.

She knew what was coming. She would be staying in this cabin for at least a few days with the man who'd introduced himself by pointing his rifle at her. Should she be more upset about that?

Probably.

But after they'd gotten past those terrifying first minutes when she'd feared he might shoot her, things had definitely started looking up. He was a good patient, and he seemed kind-hearted beneath that gruff exterior.

And this situation? It felt less like an ordeal and more like an adventure. As if she'd fallen out of her own thoroughly depressing life—

and into a weird and wonderful Christmassy escapade.

Stuck in a one-room cabin with a big, buff injured stranger for Christmas?

She'd take that over her real life any day of the week.

As it turned out, she didn't need the car key. Matthias had left the Jeep unlocked.

And there were treasures in there—three large boxes of groceries. Fresh stuff, greens and tomatoes. Apples. Bananas. Eggs, milk and cheese. A gorgeous rib roast, a fat chicken and some really pretty pork chops.

It was a good thing she'd decided to bring it all in, too. By morning everything would have been frozen.

She carried the food in first, then his laptop, a box of brightly wrapped Christmas gifts probably from his family and another boxful of books, as well.

After the boxes, she brought in three duffel bags containing men's clothes and fresh linens. Detouring to the bathroom, she stacked the linens in the cabinet. She carried the bags of clothes up to the loft, leaving them near the top of the stairs for him to deal with when he felt better.

Her sick, surly stranger definitely needed some chicken soup. She hacked up the chicken. She put the pieces on to simmer in a pot of water with onions and garlic, a little celery and some spices from the cute little spice rack mounted on the side of a cabinet.

The night wore on. She fished the cooked chicken from the pot. Once it was cool enough to handle, she got rid of the bones, chopped the meat and returned it to the pot, along with some potatoes and carrots.

On the sofa, Matthias tossed and turned, sometimes muttering to the guys named Nelson and Mark, even crying out once or twice. She soothed him when he startled awake and stroked his sweaty face with a cold cloth.

When the soup was ready, she fed it to him. He ate a whole bowlful, looking up at her through only slightly dazed blue eyes as she spooned it into his mouth. Once he'd taken the last spoonful, he said, "I've changed my mind. You can stay."

"Good. Because no one's leaving this cabin for at least a couple of days. It's seriously snowing."

"Didn't I warn you?"

"Yes, you did. And it's piling up fast, too. You're gonna be stuck with me through Christmas, anyway."

"It's all right. I can deal with you." He sat up suddenly. Before she could order him to lie back down, he said, "I really need to take a whiz—get me the cane from that basket by the door, would you?"

"You need more than a cane right now. You can lean on me."

His expression turned mulish. "You're amazing and I'm really glad you broke into my cabin. But as for staggering to the head, I can do it on my own. Get me the damn cane."

"If you tear any of your stitches falling on your ass—"

"I won't. The cane."

She gave in. *He* wasn't going to. The cane was handmade of some hard, dark wood, with a rough-hewn bear head carved into the handle. She carried it back to him. "Still here and happy to help," she suggested.

"I can manage." He winced as he swung his feet to the floor and then he looked up at her, waiting.

She got the message loud and clear. Pausing only to push the coffee table well out of his way, she stepped aside.

He braced one hand on the cane and the other on the sofa arm and dragged himself upright. It took him a while and he leaned heavily on the cane, but he made it to the bathroom and back on his own.

Once he was prone on the couch again, he allowed her to tuck the afghan in around him. She gave him more painkillers. Fifteen minutes later, he was sound asleep.

By then, it was past three in the morning. She checked her phone and found text messages—from her dad and also from Iris and Peyton, her best friends in Portland. They all three knew that it had ended with her fiancé, James. She hadn't shared the gory details with her dad, but she'd told her BFFs everything. The texts asked how she was doing, if she was managing all right?

They—her friends and her dad—believed she was spending the holiday on her own at the farm. However, with no one there but her, the farmhouse had seemed to echo with loneliness, so she'd told Nils and Marjorie Wilson, who worked and lived on the property, that she was leaving. She'd thrown her stuff in her Subaru and headed back to Portland, stopping off at the fish hatchery on the spur of the moment.

And ending up stranded in a cabin in the woods with a stranger named Matthias.

Really, it was all too much to get into via text. She was safe and warm with plenty of food—and having a much better time than she'd had alone at the farmhouse. There was nothing anyone could do for her right now. They would only freak out if she tried to explain where she was and how she'd gotten there.

Sabra wished them each a merry Christmas.

She mentioned that it was snowing heavily and implied to her girlfriends that she was still at the farm and might be out of touch for a few days due to the storm. To her dad, she wrote that she'd gone back to Portland—it wasn't a lie, exactly. She *had* gone. She just hadn't gotten there yet.

Though cell service in the forest was spotty at best, a minor miracle occurred and all three texts went through instantly—after which she second-guessed herself. Because she probably ought to tell someone that she was alone with a stranger in the middle of the woods.

But who? And to what real purpose? What would she even say?

Okay, I'm not exactly where I said I was. I'm actually snowed in at an isolated cabin surrounded by the Clatsop State Forest with some guy named Matthias Bravo, who's passed out on the sofa due to illness and injury...

No. Uh-uh. She'd made the right decision in

the first place. Why worry them when there was nothing they could do?

She powered off the phone to save the battery and wandered upstairs, where she turned on the lamps on either side of the bed and went looking for the Christmas decorations Matthias had to have somewhere.

Score! There were several plastic tubs of them stuck in a nook under the eaves. She carried them downstairs and stacked them next to that gorgeous tree.

By then, she was yawning. All of a sudden, the energy had drained right out of her. She went back to the loft and fell across the bed fully clothed.

Sabra woke to gray daylight coming in the one tiny window over the bed—and to the heavenly smell of fresh coffee.

With a grunt, she pushed herself to her feet and followed her nose down to the main floor and the coffee maker on the counter. A clean mug waited beside it. Matthias must have set it out for her, which almost made her smile.

And Sabra Bond never smiled before at least one cup of morning coffee.

Once the mug was full, she turned and leaned against the counter to enjoy that first, all-important sip.

Matthias was sitting up on the sofa, his bad leg stretched out across the cushions, holding a mug of his own, watching her. "Rough night, huh?"

She gave him her sternest frown. "You should not have been up and you are not allowed to speak to me until I finish at least one full cup of coffee."

He shrugged. But she could tell that he was trying not to grin.

She took another big gulp. "Your face is still flushed. That means you still have a fever."

He sipped his coffee and did not say a word. Which was good. Great. Exactly what she'd asked for.

She knocked back another mouthful. "At least you're not sweating anymore. Have you taken more acetaminophen since last night?"

He regarded her with mock gravity and slowly shook his head in the negative.

She set down her mug, grabbed a glass, filled it with water and carried it over to him. "There you go. Take your pills. I'll need to check your bandage and then I'll cook us some breakfast."

He tipped his golden head down and looked at her from under thick, burnished eyebrows. His mouth kept twitching. Apparently, he was finding her extremely amusing.

"What?" she demanded.

He only shook his head again.

She marched back to the counter, leaned

against it once more and enjoyed the rest of her coffee in blessed silence.

"You don't happen to have an extra toothbrush, by any chance?" she asked once she'd drained the last drop from the mug. He just gave her more silent smirking. "Oh, stop it. You may speak."

"You're such a charmer in the morning."

She grunted. "Toothbrush?"

"Under the bathroom sink. Small plastic tub. There should be a couple of them still in the wrappers and some of those sample-sized tubes of toothpaste."

"Thank you—need more coffee before I go in there? Because I am completely serious. For today at least, you're not getting up unless you really need to."

He set his mug on the coffee table and reached for the bottle of painkillers. "No more coffee right now. I'll have another cup with breakfast."

The fire was all but out. She added a little kindling and another log. As soon as the flames licked up, she faced him. "Do not get up from that couch while I'm in there."

He was stretched out on his back again, adjusting the afghan, but he dropped it to make a show of putting his hands up in surrender. "I will not move from this spot until you give me permission."

She grabbed her pack. "That's what I wanted to hear."

In the bathroom, she didn't even glance at the mirror. Not at first. The coffee had gone right to her bladder, so she took care of that. It wasn't until she stood at the sink to wash her hands that she saw what Matthias had been trying not to laugh about.

She had three deep sleep wrinkles on the left side of her face and her hair was smashed flat on that side, with another ratty-looking section of it standing straight up from the top of her head.

A little grooming was definitely in order. She took off her clothes and gave herself a quick sponge bath, after which she brushed her teeth, put her clothes back on and combed her hair, weaving it into a single braid down her back.

By then, she almost looked human.

Snow had piled up on the sill outside the tiny bathroom window. She went on tiptoe to peer through the clear part of the glass.

A blanket of unbroken white extended, smooth and sparkly, to the tree line. The trees themselves were more white than green. And it was still coming down.

Everything out that window looked brand-new. And she felt…gleeful.

She had someone to spend her Christmas with. And a gorgeous tree to decorate.

So what if that someone was a stranger and the tree wasn't hers? This totally unexpected interlude in the forest was just fine with her. She felt energized, very close to happy. And ready for anything.

For the first time in a long time, she looked forward with real anticipation to whatever was going to happen next.

Chapter Three

Matt was feeling almost human again. Yeah, his leg ached a little. But he'd taken his temperature before he made the coffee. It was down two degrees. His headache was gone.

Sabra came out of the bathroom looking a lot more pulled together than when she'd gone in. Though really, she'd been damn cute with her hair sticking up every which way, giving him the evil eye, ordering him to keep his mouth shut until she'd had her coffee.

"How about some oatmeal?" she asked as she refilled his coffee mug. "Think you could keep that down?"

He had zero desire to eat mush. "Did I dream it or did you haul everything in from the Jeep last night?"

"No dream. I brought the food and your other things inside."

"And you made soup."

"Yes, I did."

"It was delicious. I can't tell you how much I appreciate everything you've done and I would like eggs, bacon and toast. Please."

She handed him the mug and then stood above him, holding the coffee carafe, her head tipped to the side as she studied him. "I'm not going to be happy with you if it all comes right back up." She put on her don't-mess-with-me look, just to let him know who was boss.

Damn. The woman had attitude. And she

took care of business. She was tough and resourceful and pretty much unflappable—with a dry sense of humor.

Not to mention she looked amazing in panties and a sports bra.

Matt liked her. A lot. He was a little blown away at how much. As a rule, he was cautious around new people. But for her, he would definitely make an exception. He said what he was thinking. "I could have done a lot worse than to get snowed in with you."

For that, he got a small nod and a hint of a smile. "I'm glad you're feeling better. I just want you to be careful not to overdo it."

"Eggs," he said longingly. "Toast. Bacon."

She made a disapproving face, but then she cooked him the breakfast he asked for. He did his part and kept the food down. After the meal, she changed his bandage. His leg wasn't pretty, but there was no sign of infection.

Once she'd changed the dressing, she got him some sweats and clean underwear from the duffel bags she'd brought in from the car. She even allowed him to hobble into the bathroom on his own steam.

He brushed his teeth, cleaned himself up a little and changed into the stuff she'd brought downstairs for him. When he emerged into the main room, she said he looked a little green and ordered him to lie down.

"I have a request," she said as she tucked the old afghan in around him.

"My Jeep? My bank account number? The deed to this cabin? Whatever you want from me, it's yours."

She laughed. The sound was low and a little bit husky. Every time she bent close, he could smell her. She'd used the Ivory soap in the bathroom, yeah, but beneath that, her body itself smelled clean and sweet, like fresh-baked bread or maybe sugar cookies. Sugar cookies and woman.

A knockout combination.

Really, she had it all going on. He'd never realized before that he might have a type. *Hi, I'm Matt Bravo and I like my women hot, smart, competent and bossy.* As soon as he was capable of washing up in the bathroom without needing a nap afterward, it was going to get really difficult not to put a move on her.

Now, though? He was weak as a baby and fading fast, making her one-hundred-percent safe from his bad intentions.

"Keep your bank account," she said with a grin. "It's your tree I'm after."

He imagined reaching up, running a finger down the velvety skin of her neck, maybe tugging on that thick braid down her back—and what was this he was feeling? Like he had a crush on her or something.

Matt didn't do crushes. He'd been in love once and it had all gone to hell like everything else in his life at that time. Nowadays, he went out occasionally with women who wanted the same thing he did—satisfying sex. And no sleeping over.

Although, in all honesty, if he was going to crush on a woman, it would have to be this one.

"Matthias? You okay?"

He picked up the conversation where he'd dropped it. "I noticed you found the decorations and brought them down."

She grinned. "It's Christmas Eve. You're in no condition to decorate that tree and it's not going to decorate itself. Is it all right with you if I do it?"

She was way too much fun to tease. "You sure you don't want the Jeep? It's a Rubicon. Super fancy. You can go off-road in it, take a seventy-degree downhill grade on rugged terrain without even stopping to consider the risks—because there are none."

A sound escaped her, a snappy little "Ffft." She gave him a light slap on the shoulder with the back of her hand. "Stop messing with me. Say yes."

He stared up into those beautiful brown eyes. "Yes."

"Well, all right." She retucked a bit of his blanket. "That wasn't so hard, was it?"

He reached back and punched his pillow a little, all for show. "Have fun."

"I will."

"And try to keep the noise down. I need my sleep." He turned his head toward the back of the sofa and closed his eyes.

But not two minutes later, he rolled his head back the other way so he could watch her work.

Methodical and exacting, that was her tree-decorating style. She found the lights, plugging in each string first, replacing the few bulbs that had gone out. There weren't many bad bulbs because Matt took care of his gear. Also, the lights weren't that old.

This was his third Christmas at the cabin. His great-uncle Percy Valentine had given the place to him when Matt was discharged from the service. *A few wooded acres and a one-room cabin, Matthias*, Uncle Percy had said. *I'm thinking it will be a quiet place just for you, a place where you can find yourself again.*

Matt wasn't all that sure he'd found himself yet, but he liked having his own place not far from home to go when he needed it. He had a large family and they kept after him to start showing up for Christmas, which had always been a big deal for all of them.

His mom had loved Christmas and she used to do it up right. She and his dad had died when Matt was sixteen, but his older brother Daniel had stepped up, taken custody of all of them and continued all the family Christmas traditions.

He loved them, every one of them. He would do just about anything for them. But for Christmas, he liked the cabin better. He liked going off into a world of his own now and then, needed it even. Especially for the holidays. There was something about this time of the year that made the ghosts of his past most likely to haunt him.

Through half-closed eyes, he watched as Sabra strung the lights. She tucked them in among the thick branches just so, making sure there were no bare spaces, the same way he would have done. When she neared the top, she found the folding footstool in the closet under the stairs and used it to string those lights all the way up.

She had the lights on and was starting to hang ornaments when his eyes got too heavy to keep open even partway. Feeling peaceful and damn close to happy, he drifted off to sleep.

When he woke again, Sabra was curled in a ball in the old brown armchair across from the sofa, asleep. She'd found a book, no doubt from the bookcase on the side wall. It lay open across her drawn-up thighs, her dark head drooping over it.

The tree was finished. She'd done a great job of it. He just lay there on the sofa and admired it for a few minutes, tall and proud, shining so bright. She'd even put his presents from the family under it.

But he was thirsty and his water glass was empty. He sat up and reached for the cane that he'd propped at the end of the sofa.

That small movement woke her. "Wha...?"

She blinked at him owlishly. "Hey. You're awake." She rubbed the back of her neck.

He pushed back the afghan and brought his legs to the floor. "The tree is gorgeous."

She smiled, a secret, pleased little smile. "Thanks. How're you feeling?"

"Better." He pushed himself upright and she didn't even try to stop him.

"You look better. Your color's good. Want some soup?"

"If I can sit at the table to eat it."

"You think you're up for that?"

"I know I am."

Matthias *was* better. Lots better.

So much better that, after dinner that night, when he wanted to go out on the porch, she agreed without even a word of protest.

"You'll need a warmer coat," he said, and sent her upstairs to get one of his.

The coat dwarfed her smaller frame. On her, it came to midthigh and the arms covered her hands. She loved it. It would keep her toasty warm even out in the frozen night air—and it smelled like him, of cedar and something kind of minty.

On the porch, there were two rustic-looking log chairs. Sabra pushed the chairs closer together and they sat down.

The snow had finally stopped. They'd gotten several feet of the stuff, which meant they would definitely be stuck here for at least the next few days.

Sabra didn't mind. She felt far away from her real life, off in this silent, frozen world with a man who'd been a stranger to her only the day before.

He said, "My mom used to love the snow. It doesn't snow that often in Valentine Bay, but when it did she would get us all out into the yard to make snowmen. There was never that much of it, so our snowmen were wimpy ones. They melted fast."

"You're from Valentine Bay, then?" Valentine Bay was on the coast, a little south of Warrenton, which was at the mouth of the Columbia River.

He turned to look at her, brow furrowing. "Didn't I tell you I'm from Valentine Bay?"

"You've told me now—and you said your mom *used* to love the snow?"

"That's right. She died eleven years ago. My dad, too. In a tsunami in Thailand, of all the crazy ways to go."

"You've lost both of them? That had to be hard." She wanted to reach out and hug him. But that would be weird, wouldn't it? She felt like she knew him. But she didn't, not really. She needed to try to remember to respect the guy's space.

"It was a long time ago. My oldest brother Daniel took over and raised us the rest of the way. He and his wife Lillie just continued right on, everything essentially the way it used be, including the usual Christmas traditions. Even now, they all spend Christmas day at the house where we grew up. They open their presents together, share breakfast and cook a big Christmas dinner."

"But you want to spend your Christmas alone."

"That's right."

A minute ago, she'd been warning herself to respect the man's space. Too bad. Right now, she couldn't resist trying to find out more. "Last night, you were talking in your sleep."

He gave her a long look. It wasn't an encouraging one. "Notice the way I'm not asking what I said?"

"Don't want to talk about Mark and Nelson and Finn?"

He didn't. And he made that perfectly clear—by changing the subject. "You said you grew up on a farm?"

"Yes, I did."

"Near here, you said?"

"Yeah. Near Svensen."

"That's in Astoria."

"Yeah, pretty much."

"But you were headed for Portland when you suddenly decided on a hike to the falls?"

"I live in Portland now. I manage the front of the house at a restaurant in the Pearl." The Pearl District was the right place to open an upscale, farm-to-table restaurant. Delia Mae's was one of those.

"Got tired of farming?" His breath came out as fog.

She gathered his giant coat a little closer

around her against the cold. "Not really. I'm a farmer by birth, vocation and education. I've got a bachelor's degree in environmental studies with an emphasis in agroecology."

"From UC Santa Cruz, am I right?"

"The Slugs hat and sweatshirt?"

"Dead giveaway." He smiled, slow and sexy, his white, even teeth gleaming in the porch light's glow. She stared at him, thinking that he really was a hot-looking guy, with those killer blue eyes, a shadow of beard scruff on his sculpted jaw and that thick, unruly dark blond hair.

And what were they talking about?

Farming. Right. "Our farm has been in the Bond family for generations. My dad and mom were a true love match, mutually dedicated to each other, the farm and to me, their only child. All my growing-up years, the plan was for me to work right along with them, and to take the reins when the time came. But then, when I was nineteen and in my first year at Santa Cruz, my mom died while driving home from a quick shopping trip into downtown Astoria on a gray day in February. Her pickup lost traction on the icy road. The truck spun out and crashed into the guardrail."

Matthias didn't even hesitate. He reached out between their two chairs, clasped her shoulder with his large, strong hand and gave a nice, firm squeeze. They shared a glance, a long one that made her feel completely understood.

His reassuring touch made it all the easier to confess, "I have a hard time now, at the farm. It's been six years since my mom died, but my dad has never really recovered from the loss. I guess, to be honest, neither have I. After college, I just wanted something completely different."

"And now you run a restaurant."

"The chef would disagree. But yeah. I manage the waitstaff, the hiring, supervising and scheduling, all that."

He shifted in the hard chair, wincing a little.

"Your leg is bothering you," she said. "We should go in."

"I like it out here." He seemed to be studying her face.

"What?"

"I like *you*, Sabra." From the snow-covered trees, an owl hooted. "I like you very much, as a matter of fact."

A little thrill shivered through her. She relished it. And then she thought about James. She'd almost married him less than a week ago. It was turning out to be much too easy to forget him.

"What'd I say?" Matthias looked worried.

"Something nice. Too bad I'm not looking for anything remotely resembling romance."

"It's not a problem," he said in that matter-of-fact way of his. "Neither am I."

She felt a flash of disappointment, and quickly banished it. "Excellent. No romance. No…fooling around. None of that. We have a deal."

He nodded. "Agreed. And I sense a story here. You should tell it to me."

"Though you won't tell me yours?"

"I'm sure yours is more interesting than mine." Again, he shifted. His leg hurt. He just refused to admit it.

"I'm braver than you, Matthias."

He didn't even try to argue the point. "I have no doubt that you are."

"I'll put it right out there, tell you all about my failures in love."

He looked at her sideways. "You're after something. What?"

She laughed. "I'm not telling you anything until you come back inside."

In the cabin, they hung their coats by the door. Matt took off his boots and settled on the sofa with his bad leg stretched out.

"You want some hot chocolate or something?" she offered.

Was she stalling? He wanted that story. He gestured at the armchair. "Sit. Start talking."

She laughed that husky laugh of hers. The sound made a lightness inside him. She was something special, all right. And this was suddenly turning out to be his favorite Christmas ever.

She took off her own boots, filled his water glass for him and put another log on the fire.

Finally, she dropped into the brown chair

across the coffee table from him. "Okay. It's like this. I've been engaged twice. The first time was at Santa Cruz. I fell hard for a bass-playing philosophy major named Stan."

"I already hate him."

"Why?"

"Was he your first lover?" As soon as he asked, he wished he hadn't. A question like that could be considered to be crossing a certain line.

But she didn't seem turned off by it. "How did you know?"

"Just a guess—and I'm not sure yet why I hate him. Because I like *you*, I think, and I know it didn't last with him. I'm guessing that was all his fault."

"I don't want to be unfair to Stan."

Matt laughed. It came out sounding rusty. He wasn't a big laugher, as a rule. "Go ahead.

Be unfair to Stan. There's only you and me here. And I'm on *your* side."

"All right, fine." She gave a single, definitive nod. "Please feel free to hate him. He claimed to love me madly. He asked me to marry him."

"Let me guess. You said yes."

"Hey. I was twenty-one. Even though losing my mom had rocked the foundations of my world, I still had hopes and dreams back then."

"Did you move in together?"

"We did. We had this cute apartment not far from the ocean and we were planning an earthcentric wedding on a mountaintop."

"But the wedding never happened."

"No, it did not. Because one morning, I woke up alone. Stan had left me a note."

"Don't tell me the note was on his pillow."

Stifling a giggle, she nodded.

"Okay, Sabra. Hit me with it. What did the note say?"

"That he couldn't do it, couldn't marry me. Marriage was just too bougie, he wrote."

"*Bougie?* He wrote that exact word?" At her nod, he said, "And you wondered why I hate Stan."

"He also wrote that I was a good person, but I didn't really crank his chain. He had to follow his bliss to Austin and become a rock star."

"What a complete douchebasket."

"Yeah, I guess he was, kind of."

"*Kind* of? People shouldn't make promises they don't mean to keep."

Sabra sat forward in the big brown armchair.

Was he speaking from painful experience? She really wanted to know. But he didn't want to talk about himself—not as of now, anyway.

And those deep blue eyes had turned wary, as though he guessed she was tempted to ask him a question he wouldn't answer.

"Keep talking," he commanded. "What happened after Stan?"

"After Stan, I decided that my judgment about men was out of whack and I swore to myself I wouldn't get serious with a guy until I was at least thirty."

Now he was looking at her sideways, a skeptical sort of look. "Thirty, huh?"

"That's right."

"And as of today, you are…?"

"Twenty-five," she gave out grudgingly.

"And why am I thinking you've broken your own rule and gotten serious since Stan?"

"Don't gloat, Matthias. It's not attractive— and you know, I kind of can't believe I'm telling you all this. I think I've said enough."

"No. Uh-uh. You have to tell me the rest."

"Why?"

"Uh." His wide brow wrinkled up. "Because I'm an invalid and you are helping me through this difficult time."

She couldn't hold back a snort of laughter. "I really think you're going to survive whether I tell you about James or not."

"So. The next guy's name is James?"

She groaned. "The *next* guy? Like there've been a hundred of them?"

He sat very still. She could practically see the wheels turning inside his big head. "Wait. I think that came out wrong."

"No, it didn't. Not at all. I'm just messing with you."

"You're probably thinking I'm a jerk just like Stan." He looked so worried about that. She wanted to grab him and hug him and tell him everything was fine—and that was at least the second time tonight she'd considered putting her hands on him for other than purely medical reasons.

It had to stop.

"No," she said. "I honestly don't think you're a jerk—and look, Matthias, I've been meaning to ask you…"

Matthias *felt* like a jerk, whether or not Sabra considered him one. He'd been having a great time with her, like they'd known each other forever.

Until he went and put his foot in it. As a rule, he was careful around women. He wasn't ready for anything serious, so he watched himself, made sure he didn't give off the wrong signals.

But Sabra. Well, already she was kind of getting under his skin. There was so damn much to admire about her—*and* she was fun. And hot.

But they'd agreed that the man/woman thing wasn't happening. He was friend-zoned and he could live with that. Anything more, well…

It would be too easy to fall for her. And he didn't want to fall for anyone. Not yet. Maybe never. The last year or so, he'd finally started to feel like his life was back on track. True, getting something going with a woman could turn out to be the best thing that ever happened to him.

But it might send him spinning off the rails.

He just wasn't ready to find out which.

"Do you maybe have some sweats I could wear?" she asked. "Something soft to sleep in would be great…"

She was going to bed now? It wasn't much past nine.

No doubt about it. He'd definitely screwed up.

"Uh, sure," he said, and tried not to let his

disappointment show. "Take anything you want from whatever's upstairs."

"I was thinking I might even have a bath, if that's all right with you?"

"Now?"

"Well, I mean, no time like the present, right?"

"Absolutely. Go ahead."

She got up. "Can I get you anything before I—?"

"No. Really. I'm good."

She took off up the stairs. Not five minutes later, she came running back down with an armful of his clothes and disappeared into the bathroom.

He sat there and stared at the tree and tried not to imagine what she was doing behind that shut door. Really, he must be getting better fast—he had the erection to prove it.

Friend-zoned, you idiot. And that's how you want it.

He needed to take his mind off his exceptionally clear mental image of Sabra, naked in the tub, her almost-black hair piled up on her head, random strands curling in the steam rising from the water, clinging to the silky skin of her neck as she raised one of those gorgeous long legs of hers and braced her foot on the side of the tub.

Lazily, humming a holiday tune under her breath, she would begin to work up a lather. Soap bubbles would dribble slowly along her inner thigh…

Matt swore, a graphic string of bad words.

And then he grabbed his cane and shot to his feet, only swaying a little as his bad leg took his weight—yeah, he'd promised her he would stay on the sofa unless he had a good reason to get up.

Well, clearing his mind of certain way-too-tempting images was a good enough reason for him.

He limped over to the bookcase. She'd set the box of books he'd brought from home right there in the corner on the floor.

Might as well shelve them. He got to work, his leg complaining a little when he bent down to grab the next volume. But it wasn't that painful and it kept his mind from wandering to places it had no business going.

He was three-quarters of the way through the box when the bathroom door opened.

"Matthias. What the—? You promised you'd stay off your feet."

Yep. He could already smell the steaminess from across the room—soap and wet and heat and woman.

"Matthias?"

Slowly, so as not to make a fool of himself

lurching on his bad leg and proving how right she was that he shouldn't be on his feet, he turned to her.

Cutest damn thing he ever saw.

She was covered head to toe, dwarfed by his Clatsop Community College sweatshirt and a pair of his sweatpants she must have rolled at the waist, his red-toed work socks like clown shoes on her narrow feet.

Damn it to hell, she looked amazing, all rosy and soft, swimming in his clothes—and she'd washed her hair, too. It was still wet, curling sweetly on her shoulders.

His throat felt like it had a log stuck in it. He gave a quick cough to clear it. "I, um, just thought I might as well get these books out of the box."

She simply looked at him, shaking her head.

"C'mon," he coaxed. "I'm doing fine. It's not that big a deal."

She pressed her soft lips together—hiding a smile or holding back more scolding words? He couldn't tell which. But then she said, "I washed out my things. They're hanging over the tub and the shower bar. Hope that's okay."

"You don't even need to ask."

"All right, then."

A silence. Not an awkward one, surprisingly. She regarded him almost fondly—or was that pure wishful thinking on his part?

She spoke first. "Thought I would grab a book or two, read myself to sleep."

He wanted to beg, *Stay. Talk to me some more.* But all he said was, "Help yourself."

Big socks flapping, she crossed the room to him and made her choices as he just stood there between the box and the bookcase, breathing in the steamy scent of her, wishing she would move closer so he could smell her better.

She chose a thriller and a love story set in

the Second World War that had won a bunch of literary awards a few years ago. "Okay, then," she said finally. "Anything else I can do before I go? Shall I unplug the tree?"

"Nope. I'm almost done here. Then I'll lie down, I promise."

"Fair enough." Both books tucked under one arm, she turned for the stairs.

He bent to grab another volume, shelved it, bent to grab the next.

"Matthias?" He straightened and turned. She'd made it to the top. "Merry Christmas."

He stared up at her, aching for something he didn't want to name, feeling equal parts longing and gladness—longing for what he knew he wouldn't have.

Gladness just to be here in his cabin in the forest, stranded. With her.

"Merry Christmas, Sabra."

She granted him a smile, a slow one. And then she turned and vanished from his sight.

Chapter Four

Christmas day, Sabra woke to morning light streaming in the loft window. She could smell coffee, which meant that Matthias had been on his feet again.

She went downstairs scowling. But that was more her natural precoffee face than disapproval. The tree was lit up, looking fabulous. He was sitting on the sofa, his laptop across his stretched-out legs, apparently not in pain, his color excellent.

He'd left a mug waiting for her by the coffee maker, same as yesterday. She filled it and drank it just the way she liked it, without a word spoken.

Once it was empty, she set the mug on the counter. "Did you happen to take your temperature?"

He ran his thumb over the touch pad. "Normal."

"You have internet on that laptop?"

He tipped his head toward his phone on the coffee table. "Not using it now—but yeah, when I need it. Mobile data through my cell. It's a little spotty here in the middle of nowhere, but it works well enough." He looked up and smiled at her. Bam! The gray winter morning just got a whole lot brighter. "I also have a speaker. We can have Christmas music."

"How wonderful is that?" She wandered

over to see what game he was playing. "Soli-taire?"

"It's mindless. I find it calming." He won a game and the cards flew around and settled to start over.

She went on into the bathroom, where her clothes weren't quite dry yet and her hair looked almost as bad as it had the morning before.

After breakfast, Matthias said he wanted a real bath. She went into the bathroom first, gathered up her things and took them upstairs, after which she found a roll of plastic wrap and waterproofed his bandaged lower leg.

He hobbled into the bathroom and didn't come out for an hour. When he finally emerged smelling of toothpaste and sham-poo, she checked his stitches. There was no swelling and less redness than the day before.

"Lookin' good," she said.

"Great. I'm putting on the tunes." He used a cable to hook up his speaker to his phone. Christmas music filled the cabin.

She insisted that he open his presents. "Just sit there," she said, "nice and comfy on the couch. I'll bring them to you."

"That doesn't seem fair."

"If I'm happy doing it, it's fair enough."

His presents were the stuff guys get from their families at Christmas. Shirts and socks and a nice heavy jacket. A humorous coffee mug. Gift cards. More books.

Sabra enjoyed the process. For the first time since her mom died, she was loving every minute of Christmas. Sitting out on the porch in the freezing cold, coming downstairs in the morning to the coffee Matthias had already made though she'd ordered him not to—

everything, all of it, seemed sparkly and fresh, entertaining and baggage-free.

When the last gift card had been stripped of its shiny wrapper and pretty ribbons, he said, "There's one more under there somewhere."

"You sure? I think that's all."

"I'll find it." He reached for his bear-headed cane.

"Nope. Sit." She got down on hands and knees and peered through the thick tiers of branches. "I see it." It was tucked in close to the trunk. Pulling it free, she sat back on her heels. The snowman wrapping paper was wrinkled and the bow was made of household twine. "I don't remember this one."

"I had to make do with what I found in the kitchen drawers."

"It's for me?" Her throat kind of clutched. Maybe. A little.

"Yeah—and don't make a big deal of it or

start in on how I shouldn't have been on my feet."

She slanted him a sideways look. "Lotta rules you got when it comes to giving someone a present, Matthias."

"It's Christmas. I wanted you to have *something*, okay?"

"Um. Okay." She gazed at him steadily, thinking what a great guy he was under the gruffness and self-protective, macho-man bluster.

"It's nothing," he mumbled. "Just open it."

Oh, she definitely was tempted to dish out a little lecture about how a guy should never call any gift "nothing." But then he would consider that making a "big deal." Better not to even get started. She untied the twine bow and tore off the wrinkled paper.

Inside was a See's Candy box and inside that, a folded piece of paper bag and a small, roughly carved wooden animal. "It's so cute." She held it up. "A hedgehog?"

"Close. A porcupine. I made it last night, sitting out on the porch after you went to bed."

She started to chide him for not going to sleep early as he'd promised—but then pressed her lips together before any words escaped. His gift touched her heart and being out on the porch for a while didn't seem to have hurt him any.

He said, "Me and my Swiss Army knife, we have a great time together."

She turned the little carving in her hands, admiring his work. "I love it. Truly. Thank you."

He gave a one-shouldered shrug. "I thought you might want a souvenir, something to remind you of all that can happen if you go wandering into the woods at Christmastime. You could end up facing down a crazy man with a gun and then having to perform emergency surgery." He grinned.

She felt an answering smile lift the corners of her mouth. "Why a porcupine?"

"No reason, really. I got out my knife and a nice bit of wood that was just the right shape to become a porcupine."

"Great choice. I'm a porcupine sort of girl—kinda prickly."

"But cute."

Was she blushing? God. Probably. "Did you make your cane?" She tipped her head toward where it leaned against the end of the sofa.

"Yes, I did."

She had that urge again—to jump up and hug him. Again, she resisted it. But her defenses were weakening. The more time she spent with him, the more she wanted to touch him, to have him touch her.

Shifting her legs out from under her, she sat

cross-legged on the floor, set the sweet little porcupine beside her and unfolded the paper-bag note.

Merry Christmas, Sabra,

I'll make your coffee whether you allow me to or not. And I'll shut up while you drink it. Feel free to break into my cabin anytime.

Matthias

She glanced up to find him watching her. "You realize you just gave me an open invitation to invade your forest retreat whenever the mood strikes."

He gazed at her so steadily. "Anytime. I mean that."

Did she believe him? Not really. But still, it pleased her no end that he seemed to like having her around.

* * *

It was a great Christmas, Matt thought, easy and lazy. No tension, zero drama.

They roasted the prime rib he'd brought and sat down to dinner in the early afternoon. There was time on the porch to enjoy the snowy clearing and the tall white-mantled trees. He had board games and they played them. She won at Scrabble. He kicked her pretty butt at Risk.

Not long after dark, as they were considering a game of cribbage, the power went out. She got the footstool from under the stairs and handed him down the two boxes of candles he kept ready and waiting on top of the kitchen cabinets. They lit the candles, set them around the room and ended up abandoning the cribbage board, gravitating to their usual places instead—Matt on the sofa, Sabra curled up in the brown easy chair.

He felt comfortable enough with her to bring up the awkwardness the night before. "I really didn't mean to insult you last night—you know, what I said about you and that guy named James…"

She gave him a look he was already coming to recognize, sort of patient. And tender. "I told you that I wasn't insulted."

"But then you jumped to your feet and ran and hid in the bathroom."

"Did not," she said sharply. "I took a *bath*." She huffed out a breath. "Please."

He said nothing. He was getting to know her well enough to have a general idea of when to keep his mouth shut around her, let her come to the truth at her own speed.

And she did, first shifting in the chair, drawing her legs up the other way, wrapping her slim arms around them. "I thought maybe I was getting too personal, I guess."

"You weren't. If you want to tell it, I'm listening."

Her sleek eyebrows drew together as she thought it over. "It *is* helpful, to have someone to talk to. You're a good listener and this is just the right situation, you know? You and me alone in this cabin, away from the rest of the world. I think it shocked me last night, how easy it was to say hard stuff to you. You're the stranger I'll probably never see again once the roads are clear and we can go our separate ways." She swiped a hand down her shining dark hair and flicked her braid back over her shoulder.

He could sit here forever, just looking at her.

She had it right, though—yeah, he ached to kiss her. To touch her. To see where this attraction he felt for her might go.

But at the same time, he'd been careful not to tell her too much about himself, about his life. He'd come a long way in the past few years. But not far enough. He still wasn't ready to jump off into the deep end with a woman again.

And Sabra Bond? She was the kind a guy should be ready to go deep with.

Sabra hugged her knees a little closer, thinking how the man across the coffee table from her reminded her of her dad a little—her dad the way he used to be, back in the old days, before they'd lost her mom. Like her father, Matthias was self-contained. He really listened. He took her seriously but he knew how to kid around, too. He also seemed the sort of man who would tell the truth even when it hurt.

"So, where was I?" she asked.

He tipped his dark gold head to the side, considering, for several long seconds before replying. "You told me about Stan, who left in the middle of the night to move to Austin and become a rock star, the lousy bastard. What about James?"

"James. Right. After Stan, I swore off men."

"How'd that work out?"

"For a while, I had no romantic relationships of any kind. Then, in my last year at Santa Cruz, I met James Wise. James is from a wealthy Monterey family and he was studying computer game design—not really seriously, though, as it turned out."

"Right. Because…trust fund?"

"A giant one. He was fooling around with game design and his parents were constantly pressuring him to join the family real estate development firm."

"So you two were a thing, you and James?"

She nodded. "We were. He was fun and he didn't seem to take things too seriously. I was so proud of myself for finally having a no-strings sexual relationship."

"But then…?"

"After we dated for a month or two, James started pushing for marriage."

Matthias made a low, knowing sort of sound. "And you explained that you planned to be single for years yet."

"I did, yes. We split up at graduation. I moved to Portland."

"A fresh start."

"That's right. I got my own place and a job at that restaurant I told you about, where I met Iris and Peyton, who became my best friends. I kept promising my friends I would enjoy my freedom, get out and experience a few hot and sexy nights with men I never intended to spend forever with. Somehow, that never happened. And then James showed up in Portland."

"Because he couldn't live without you."

"That is exactly what he said." She turned sideways and hung her legs over the chair arm, using the other arm as a backrest, shoving a throw pillow behind her for extra support. "And how'd you know that?"

"Lucky guess. Continue."

"Well, I really had missed him. Yeah, I knew he was a little…irresponsible, maybe. But he was so romantic and sweet—and lighthearted, you know? Since my mom's death, a little lightheartedness means a lot. He kind of swept me off my feet. We got a place together and he kept pushing for marriage…"

"And you finally said yes."

"Nailed it."

"But what about those no-strings flings you promised your girlfriends you'd be having?"

"Never got around to them. And I know, the plan was I would wait till I was thirty to even get serious. Yet, somehow, there I was, saying yes to James—also, full disclosure? I'd never actually met his family or taken him to meet my dad."

"Uh-oh."

"Tell me about it." She groaned. "I ask you, could there have *been* more red flags?"

"Don't beat yourself up. It's all in the past, right?"

A little shudder went through her. "Right. The very recent past, unfortunately—but anyhow, we agreed we'd skip the fancy wedding. I'd never wanted one of those and he could not have cared less either way. We set a date for a quickie Vegas ceremony, which was to have taken place exactly six days ago today. Then after the wedding, the plan was that James would sweep me off for a Christmas vacation-slash-honeymoon in the Seychelles."

"Christmas in the tropics. That does sound romantic. Ten points for James."

"I thought so, too. And I did insist he had to at least meet my dad first, so we went to the farm for Thanksgiving."

"Did you have a nice visit?"

She narrowed her eyes at him. "Go ahead, Matthias. Pour on the irony."

"Sorry." He didn't look the least regretful.

"You're enjoying this far too much."

"I'm only teasing you—you know, being *lighthearted*?"

She pulled the pillow out from behind her back and threw it at him.

He caught it. "Whoa. Just missed the candle."

"Watch out. I'll do worse than knock over a candle."

He put the pillow under his injured leg. "So? The visit to the farm…?"

"It was bad. My dad was polite to James, but two days in, Dad got me alone and asked me if I was really sure about marrying the guy."

"Ouch. That's tough."

"And I reacted with anger. I said some mean things about how, since we'd lost Mom, he didn't care about anything—but now, all of a sudden, he's got a negative opinion he just has to share concerning my choice of a life mate."

"Admit it," Matthias interjected in that rough, matter-of-fact tone she already knew so well. "You were worried that your dad might be right."

She decided his remark didn't require a response. "After the awfulness with my dad, James and I went back to Portland."

"Your dad was right, though—am I right?"

She wished she had another pillow to throw at him. "Seven days ago, the day before we were supposed to head for Vegas, James's parents arrived out of nowhere at our apartment."

"Not good?"

"Horrible. They'd come to collect their errant son before he made the biggest mistake of his life—marrying some nobody farmer's daughter when the woman he grew up with, a woman from an excellent family, a woman who loved him with all her heart, was waiting for him in Monterey—with their little boy who needed his daddy."

"What the—? James had a kid?"

She nodded. "One he'd never said a word to me about."

"Okay, now I want to kick his snotty little rich-guy ass."

"Thank you. Anyway, James asks his parents to leave. They go. At this point, I'm reeling. I demand an explanation—and James just blurts out the truth he never bothered to share with me before. He says yes, there's a little boy. That in the year between graduation and when he showed up in Portland, he'd gotten back with his childhood sweetheart and she'd had his baby. He says he hates that maybe his parents are right. Monica—his baby mama—really does need him and so does his son. He says he's sorry, but he can't marry me and he's leaving for Monterey right away."

"Sabra."

She glared across the coffee table at him to keep from getting weepy over her terrible life choices. "What?"

"This all happened a week ago?"

"James went back to Monterey exactly one week ago today, yes."

Matthias took the pillow out from under his leg, plopped it on the coffee table and scooted around so he could rest his leg on it again.

Then he patted the space beside him. "Come here."

"Why?"

He only patted the empty cushion some more.

"Fine." She got up and sat next to him.

And he hooked his giant arm around her and pulled her close. "Lean on me. It's not going to kill you."

She let her head drop to his enormous shoulder, breathed in his minty, manly evergreen scent—and felt comforted. "Thanks."

His breath brushed the crown of her head. He might even have pressed a kiss there, though she couldn't be sure. "Continue."

"What else is there to say? I gave him back his ring and he packed a suitcase and left. I told myself to look on the bright side. I had three weeks off work for the honeymoon that wasn't happening, time off from the daily grind to pull it together, find a new place and sublet the apartment I can't afford to keep by myself."

"Plus, you'd dodged a major bullet not marrying a cheating, dumb-ass rich kid from Monterey."

"Yay, me." It felt good to be held by him. She snuggled in a little closer. When she tipped her head back to glance up at him, he bent close and touched his nose to hers, causing a sweet little shiver to radiate out from that small point of contact.

"You okay?" he asked, blue eyes narrowed with concern.

"I am," she replied, resting her head on his shoulder. "I threw some clothes in a bag and went to the farm, where my dad was still wandering around like a ghost of himself. But at least he hugged me and said he loved me and he was glad I hadn't married the wrong man.

He wanted me to come with him for Christmas with my mom's side of the family, but I wasn't up for it. After Dad left, it got really lonely at the farm, so I started back to Portland—and the rest, you know."

"Luckily for me, you ended up here in time to save my sorry ass from my own hopeless pigheadedness."

"You're welcome." She eased free of his hold to bring a knee up on the sofa cushion and turn toward him. "And at least I've learned something from the disaster that was James."

"What's that?"

"For the next five years, minimum, the only relationships I'm having are the casual kind."

He scratched his chin, pretending to think deeply about what she'd just said. "I don't know, Sabra. Isn't that what you promised yourself after things went south with Stan?

You seem to be kind of a sucker for a marriage proposal."

She was tempted to fake outrage. But really, why bother? He was absolutely right on both counts. "Yeah, I do have that teensy problem of being monogamous to the core." A sad little laugh escaped her. "It's bred in the bone with me, I guess."

"Why's that?"

"My parents fell in love when they were kids—and their dedication to each other? Absolute. I just want what they had, but so far it's not happening." Matthias was watching her with a kind of musing expression. And she felt…bold. And maybe a little bit giddy. She took it further. "I'm probably never trying love again. And I'm incapable of having casual sex with men I don't know. That means I'm doomed to spend my life only having sex with myself—and I know, I know. TMI in a big way." Matthias chuckled. It was a rough sound, that chuckle. And very attractive. She felt strangely proud every time she made him laugh. "And now that I've totally overshared the story of my pitiful love life, you sure you don't want to do a little sharing, too?"

He grunted. "Do I look like the sharing type to you?"

She didn't back down. "Yeah. You do. Talk to me about the things you said in your sleep the other night."

He went straight to tough-guy denial. "No idea what you're talking about."

"The name Nelson doesn't even ring a bell?"

"Who?" he sneered—but in a teasing kind of way that seemed to give her permission to keep pushing.

Sabra pushed. "So…you don't want to talk about Mark or Finn, either, or the woman you mentioned. Christy, I think her name was…"

He squinted at her, as though he was trying to see inside her head. "You really want to hear this crap?"

"I'm sure it's *not* crap. And yes, I really do."

"All right, then." And just like that, he gave it up. "Christy was my high school sweetheart. We were still together after a couple of years of community college. I was messing up all over the place back then, drinking, exploring the effects of a number of recreational drugs and playing video games instead of taking care of business. My issues had issues, I guess you could say. But at least I knew Christy was the love of my life."

"That's sweet."

He snorted derisively. "Wait for the rest of it. At twenty, after squeaking through my sophomore year with a C-minus average, my older brother Daniel gave me a good talking-to—a few blows were thrown. But he did get through to me. I decided to enlist, to serve my country and get my act together.

"Before I left for boot camp, I proposed and Christy said yes. We agreed to a two-year engagement so that she could finish college before the wedding. A year later, while I was overseas, she Dear Johned me via email and then married the guy she'd been cheating on me with."

"Oh, dear God, Matthias. That's bad."

"What happened with Christy was by no means the worst of it." His eyes were flat now, far away.

She felt terrible for him and almost let him off the hook. But he fascinated her. She wanted to know his story, to understand what had shaped the man he was now.

"Nelson and Mark were good men," he continued in a monotone. "We served together in the Middle East. They didn't make it home. I got discharged due to injury. I was a mess. There were surgeries and lots of therapy—

both kinds, physical and for my screwed-up head. Finn was my brother."

"Was?" she asked in a small voice, stunned by this litany of tragedy.

"It's possible he's still alive. He disappeared when he was only eight. That was my fault. I was six years older and I was supposed to be watching him. We still have investigators looking for him."

"I'm so sorry," she said, aching for him and for those he'd lost. "I really don't know what to say…"

"Don't worry about it. Can we talk about something else now, you think?"

"Absolutely."

And just like that, he shook it off and teased her, "I guess, with you being incapable of casual sex, I don't have to wonder if you took advantage of me that first night when I was at my weakest."

She followed his lead and teased him right back. "Don't look so hopeful."

"Damn. It was only a dream, then?"

"All right, I admit it." She fluttered her eyelashes madly. "For you, I have made a monogamy exception. You loved it—actually, it was good for both of us."

"I kind of figured it would be." He said that with way more sincerity than the joking moment called for.

And all of a sudden, the warm, candlelit cabin was charged with a whole new kind of heat.

Okay, yeah. The guy was super hot in his big, buff, ex-military kind of way. Plus, they'd forged a sort of instant intimacy, two strangers alone in the middle of the woods.

But getting into anything *really* intimate with him would be a bad idea. After all, she'd just gotten messed over by her second fiancé.

Having sex with Matthias would only be asking for trouble.

Wouldn't it?

Or would it be wonderful? Passionate and sweet and magical. And right.

Chemistry-wise, he really did it for her— at least, as far as she could tell without even having kissed him yet.

Why should she run from that, from the possibility of that? Maybe they could have something beautiful.

Something for right now. Just between the two of them.

Maybe, for the first time, she, Sabra Bond, could actually have a fling. That would be progress for someone like her.

They stared at each other in the flickering candlelight.

Was he just possibly thinking the same thing she was?

* * *

Sex.

Matt was definitely thinking about sex. About how much he wanted it. With the woman sitting next to him. "Sabra."

Her big eyes got bigger. "Um, yeah?"

"Whatever I say now is just going to sound like so much bull—"

She whipped up a hand. "No. No, it's not. I get you, Matthias. I do. I think, you and me, we're on the same page about this whole relationship thing. It hasn't even been a full week since I almost married a man who'd failed to tell me he had a child. I'm not ready for anything serious, not in the least. I need about a decade to figure myself out first."

"Yeah. I get that." He gave it to her straight out. "I'm not ready, either."

"But I, well, I *have* been thinking about it," she confessed. "About the two of us, here, alone. Like strangers. And yet somehow, at the same time, not strangers at all."

Were they moving too far, too fast? Yeah, probably.

He tried to lighten things up a little. "It's all the excitement and glamour, right? I mean, I know we're having a wild old time here, playing board games, sitting out on the porch watching the snow melt."

She laughed. He really liked her laugh, all husky and musical at once. But then she answered with complete sincerity. "I'm having the best time. I really am."

And what could he do but reply honestly, in kind? "Me, too." He wanted to kiss her. What man wouldn't? And as their hours together drifted by, it kept getting harder to remember why kissing her wouldn't be wise.

She got up and went back to her chair. He wanted to reach out, catch her hand, beg her to stay there on the sofa beside him. But he had no right to do any such thing.

She settled in across the coffee table, gathering her knees up against her chest, resting her pretty chin on them. "I have a proposition for you."

His heart rate picked up. "Hit me with it."

"What if we both agreed that this, right now, in this cabin at Christmas, just you and me—this is it? This is all. When it's over and we go our separate ways, that's the last we'll ever see of each other."

He felt regret, that it was going nowhere between the two of them—regret and relief in equal measure. A man needed to be realistic about what he was capable of. And what he wasn't. As for Sabra, well, she'd just gotten free of one romantic mess. A new one was the last thing she needed. "You're saying we won't be exchanging numbers?"

"That's right. No details about how to get in touch later. And no looking each other up on social media, no trying to track each other down."

"We say goodbye and walk away."

"Yes." She sat a little straighter in the chair. "What do you think?"

He stuck out his hand across the coffee table. She shifted, tucking her legs to the side, leaning forward in the chair and then reaching out to meet him.

"Deal," he said as he wrapped his fingers around hers.

Chapter Five

The second Matt released her hand, the power popped back on.

The lights flickered, and then steadied. The tree came alive, blazing bright.

"You think it'll go out again?" she asked in a whisper.

"Hell if I know." He shifted his bad leg back onto the sofa, stretching it out as before.

They sat there, waiting, for a good count of

twenty. When the lights stayed on, she bent forward to blow out the candle between them.

"Leave it for a little while, just in case," he suggested.

"Sure." She gazed across the coffee table at him—and started backing off the plan. "I, well, I just realized…" Her cheeks were bright red. She was absolutely adorable.

"Realized what?" he asked, keeping his expression serious, though inside he was grinning. Yeah, he wanted to do her ten ways to Sunday.

But if it never happened, he would still have so much—the memory of her smile, the clever bite of her sharp words. The way she only got calmer when things got scary. And how, even after he'd introduced himself by threatening her with a rifle, she'd stepped right up to do what needed doing, not only patching him up, but also taking good care of him while he was out of it.

No matter how it all turned out, this was a Christmas he wouldn't forget. Even if he never so much as kissed her, he felt a definite connection to her and he was one of those guys who didn't make connections easily.

She did some throat clearing. "It just occurred to me…"

"Yeah?"

"I don't have condoms. I'm going to take a wild guess and say you don't, either."

Wrong. Last summer he'd let Jerry Davidson, a lifelong friend, fellow game warden and self-styled player, use the cabin as a romantic getaway. Jerry had left a box of them upstairs.

"Are you getting cold feet?" he asked gently.

She scowled. "Matthias, just tell me. Do you have condoms or not?"

"I do, yeah. Upstairs in the dresser, top drawer on the right."

She blinked. "Oh. Well, okay, then—and what about your leg?"

He gave a shrug. "It could cramp my style a little, I have to admit."

"Do you want, um, to back out, then?"

He grinned. She did that to him, made him grin. Made him see the world as a better place. Made him feel comfortable in his own skin, somehow. "Not a chance."

She answered his grin with one of her own. "Then you're only saying that we should be careful, take it slow?"

"Yeah. Slow. Slow is good." He gestured at his stretched-out leg. "Slow also happens to be just about all I can manage at this point."

She leaned in a little closer. "You think you could make it up the stairs?"

"Baby, I know I could."

Her grin turned to a soft little smile. "Slowly, right?"

"That's right."

All of a sudden, she was a ball of nervous energy. She shot out of the chair. "How about some hot chocolate?"

"Sounds good." He started to get up.

"No. You stay right there. I'll get it." And she bolted for the kitchen area, where she began rattling pans. He considered following her over there for no other reason than that he liked being near her—plus, he wanted to be sure she wasn't suddenly freaking out over the plans they'd just made.

But maybe she needed a few minutes to herself. Maybe she was going to tell him that, on second thought, getting into bed with him was a bad idea.

Well, if she'd changed her mind, she would say so. No need to go looking for disappointment. If it was coming, it would find him soon enough.

He picked up his phone and got the music started again, choosing slower songs this time, Christmas ballads and easy-listening jazz.

When she returned with two mugs, she set one in front of her chair and then edged around the coffee table to put his down where he could reach it comfortably. "Here you go."

"Thanks." Before she could retreat to the other side of the table, he caught her arm in an easily breakable grip.

Her eyes widened and her mouth looked so soft and full. He couldn't wait to kiss her. "I gave you marshmallows," she said softly, like it was their secret that no one else could know.

"I love marshmallows."

"Excellent," she replied in a breathless whisper.

He exerted a gentle pressure on her arm,

pulling her down a little closer, so he could smell the clean sweetness of her skin, feel the warmth of her, imagine the beauty hidden under his baggy sweatshirt and track pants.

She didn't resist him, though she gulped hard and her breathing had grown erratic. Another quivery little smile pulled at the corners of her mouth.

One more tug was all it took. Those soft lips touched his. She sighed. The sound flowed through him. It was a happy sort of sound, warm.

Welcoming, even.

He smiled against her lips, letting go of her arm as he claimed her mouth, being careful to give her every opportunity to pull away or call a halt.

She did neither.

And he went on kissing her, keeping it light and tentative at first, brushing his lips across hers. He caught her pillowy lower lip between his teeth, biting down just enough to make her give him a little moan as he eased his fingers up over the slim curve of her shoulder.

Taking hold of her thick braid, he wrapped it around his hand, a rope of silk. She hummed into his mouth, her lips softening, giving to him, letting him in to explore the smooth, wet surfaces beyond her parted lips.

"Sabra," he whispered.

She murmured his name, "Matthias," in return.

He liked that, the way she always used his full name. Other people rarely did.

Slowly, he let the wrapped braid uncoil. That freed his hand to slip under it and clasp her nape. Her skin was warm satin, so smooth against his roughened palm. He ran his thumb and forefinger down the sides of her neck, relishing the feel of her. The fine hairs at her nape brushed at him, tickling a little in a way that both aroused him and made him smile.

He needed her closer.

Exerting gentle pressure with his hand on her nape, he guided her down to sit across his thighs.

She broke the kiss to ask, "Your leg?"

"It's fine." He caught her mouth again. She opened with a yearning little moan.

The kiss continued as he clasped her braid once more and ran his hand slowly down it. He tugged the elastic free, tossed it in the general direction of the coffee table, and then set about working his fingers through the long strands until they fell loose down her back and across her shoulders. The dark waves felt good between his fingers. They clung to his hand as he continued to kiss her slowly and thoroughly.

Letting her know that there was no rush.

That it was just the two of them, alone, together, for at least the next couple of days.

Plenty of time to explore each other, *know* each other in the best sort of way.

She pulled back, the black fans of her eyelashes lifting slowly. Her pupils had widened. She looked dazed. He probably did, too.

He leaned in to take her mouth again, a quick, hard kiss. "I can't wait to get my clothes off you."

She laughed—and then whispered, "We get to *unwrap* each other."

"Exactly."

"We are each other's Christmas present."

He pressed his forehead to hers as he ran the backs of his fingers up and down the side of her throat. "Best. Present. Ever."

She caught his jaw and held his gaze. "I love your eyes. They are the deepest, truest blue—kiss me again."

He did. She opened for him instantly and he took what she offered him, tasting her deeply, running his hands up and down her slim back, gathering her closer, so he could feel her breasts, their softness pressing against his chest.

That time, when she lifted her mouth from his, she got up. He didn't try to stop her. The whole point was not to rush.

She went and sat across the coffee table. "Drink your cocoa while it's still hot."

An hour later, the lights were still on.

He turned off the music. She blew out the candles and unplugged the tree. He grabbed the pillow she'd brought down for him that first night and followed her up the stairs.

Halfway up, she paused and glanced back at him over her shoulder. "You doing all right?"

His leg? He'd forgotten all about it. He had

more important things on his mind. "Yeah. I'm good."

She gave him a little nod and they continued on up into the loft. Through the single window, the full moon was visible, a ghostly silver disc obscured by a thin curtain of clouds.

At the bed, she flipped on one of the lamps. He passed her his pillow. She set it next to hers and turned back the blankets. He went to the dresser for the box of condoms, taking out a few, carrying them back to the far side of the bed, setting them on the nightstand.

Though she'd teased him about unwrapping each other, they didn't linger over getting their clothes off, but got right after it, tossing track pants and sweatshirts in a pile on a chair.

She was so damn pretty, slim and tight and strong, her dark hair in loose, messy curls on her shoulders.

He reached for her. She came into his arms

and she fit there just right, her skin so smooth, her eyes wide and hopeful, fluttering shut as he lowered his mouth to hers.

She tasted of hope—the kind of hope he rarely allowed himself anymore, hope for a future that included more than himself, alone, getting by. She made him feel close to her, intimate in the deepest way.

Even if it was only for right now.

Those quick, clever hands of hers caressed him, gliding up his chest, exploring, her fingers pausing to stroke their way out along his shoulders and then back in to link around his neck. "So good to kiss you," she whispered against his mouth.

"The best," he agreed. He wanted to taste every inch of her and now was his chance.

Working his way downward, he dropped nipping kisses in a trail along the side of her neck, and then in a looping pattern across her upper chest.

She murmured encouragements, her hands first cradling his face and then slipping up into his hair.

Her breasts were so beautiful, small and high, full on the underside, the nipples already hard. He tasted them, drawing them in deep as she grasped his hair tighter, holding him there, at her heart.

But there was so much more woman he needed to kiss. He kept moving, kissing on downward, dropping to his knees, not giving a damn if he split a stitch or two.

"You okay?" she asked, her head bent down to him, her hair brushing the side of his face.

"Never better." He kissed her smooth, pretty belly and then dropped more kisses around to the side of her, where he nipped at the sweetly curved bones beneath the silky flesh, feeling lost in the best kind of way—lost to the taste and smell of her.

She must have been lost, as well. Dropping her head back, she moaned at the shadowed rafters above.

"So pretty." He blew a teasing breath into the neatly trimmed sable hair at her mound, bringing his hands up to pet her a little.

"Oh!" she said. "Oh, my!" And she giggled, reaching for him, cradling his face again. She was swaying on her feet.

He caught her by the side of her hip to steady her. She felt so good, he couldn't resist sliding his hand around her, getting a big handful of her smooth round backside.

She looked down at him then, her eyes deep and dark, beckoning him. Their gazes locked. "Kiss me," she whispered. "Right there."

And he did, using his tongue, his teeth, everything, then bringing his eager hands back to the center of her, parting her for his mouth.

Already, she was slick and wet. He made her more so, darting his tongue in, licking her, then holding her still, spreading her wider with his fingers, so he could get in close and tight.

By then, she was whimpering, muttering excited encouragements. "Yes!" and "Please!" and "That! More. Oh, that…"

He gave her what she asked for, staying with her all the way, using his fingers to stroke into her. Using his tongue, too, until she went over with a low, keening cry.

He could have stayed right there on his knees forever, touching her, kissing her, petting her, whispering dark promises of all he would do to her.

But then, with a happy sigh, she dropped

back away from him onto the bed, her slim arms spread wide.

"I think I just died." She lifted her head and watched him as he braced his hands on either side of her fine thighs. "Your stitches!" she cried, that mouth he couldn't wait to kiss again forming a worried frown as he pushed himself upright.

"My stitches are just fine," he promised. "It's my knees that are shaking."

She reached up slim arms as he rose above her. "Come down here. Please. I need you close."

He went down, falling across the bed with her, catching himself on his forearms in order not to crush her completely. "I'm right here."

"And I am so glad." She touched him, learning him, her palms smoothing over his back, his shoulders, along his arms. Her fingers lingered on the ridges of scar tissue that marred his chest, neck and arms. She didn't remark on them, though.

He appreciated that.

There was nothing to say about them. He was one of the lucky ones. He'd come back from the Middle East damaged, battered—but all in one piece, after all.

He dipped close to capture her mouth again as her quick hand eased between them and encircled his hardness. When she did that, he couldn't hold back a groan.

Tightening her grip on him, she gave a little tug, bringing another rough sound from him as she pushed him onto his back and rose above him. Curving down over him, she claimed him with her mouth.

Lightning flashed along his nerve endings and the blood pumped hot and fast through his veins. She drove him just to the edge and then slacked off to tease and flick him with her tongue as she continued to work him over with those talented hands—both hands, together.

Somehow, he lasted for several minutes of that glorious torture.

But there did come a point where he had to stop her. Catching hold of her wrist, tipping up her chin with the other hand, he warned in a growl, "I'm about to go over."

She grinned, a saucy little grin. "Please do."

"Not till I'm inside you."

"But I like it. I want you to—"

"Come up here." He took her under the arms and pulled her up on top of him, so they were face-to-face, her long legs folded on either side of his body. "You are so beautiful." And then he speared his fingers into her hair, pulling it maybe a little harder than he should have. But she didn't complain.

Not Sabra. She only gave a sweet little moan and opened for his kiss.

Those idiots who'd left her?

What the hell was the matter with those two?

If she was his, he would keep her forever, keep her happy, keep her satisfied. He would never be the chump who let her go.

But she *wasn't* his.

And he needed to remember that.

Remember that neither of them was ready for anything life changing, and that was all right.

They had tonight, the next day, maybe a few days after that. They had this Christmastime with just the two of them, Sabra and Matthias, alone in his cabin in the forest.

He went on kissing her, deep and hard and endlessly, reaching out a hand for the night table and a condom. With a groan, she broke their kiss and gazed down at him through wide, wondering eyes as she lifted her slim body away from him enough for him to deal with the business of protection.

"I'll stay on top." She bent close again and scraped his scruffy jaw with her teeth. He breathed in the scent of her, so sweet, musky now. "Okay?" she asked.

"Best offer I've had in years." He groaned as she wrapped her hand around him and guided him into place. "Look at me," he whispered, as he slipped an inch inside.

She met his eyes, held them, and lowered slowly down. "Yes. Oh, yes…"

It hurt so good, her body all around him, wet and hot and so damn tight. "Sabra."

"Yes…"

She let out a sharp, pleasured cry as she took him all the way.

There was a moment of complete stillness between them. They waited, breath held. And then she moaned. She curved her body over him, her hair falling forward to caress his cheek and rub against his neck.

Then they were moving together. He pushed up into her, matching her rhythm as she picked up speed.

The way she rode him? Nothing like it. Sweet and slow and long.

Hard and fast and mercilessly. He could go forever, be with her forever, lost inside her sweetness.

Held.

Known.

Cherished.

He wanted it to last and last. Was that really so much to ask?

She seemed to understand his wish, to want it, too. For a while, they played with each other, slowing when one of them got too close to the edge, then getting swept up in the hungry glory of it all over again, going frantic and fast. She rode him so hard. He would never get enough of her, of being inside her.

Too bad they really couldn't hold out indefinitely.

He felt her climax take her, the walls of her sex clutching around him. He gritted his teeth, clasping the fine, firm curves of her hips, holding on more tightly than he should have, trying to outlast her.

By some miracle he managed it, lived through the wonder of her pulsing hard and fast around him.

When she collapsed on his chest with a sigh of happy surrender, he let go, let his finish roll through him—burning, breathtaking, overpowering. He gave himself up to it with a triumphant shout.

The snow started to melt the next day.

Sabra wished it would freeze again and stay

that way. She fantasized about being stuck in the cabin forever, just her and Matthias in a world all their own.

But the snow kept melting. By the twenty-eighth, there was nothing left of it beyond a few dirty patches dotting the clearing and the dirt road leading out. Matthias drove her to the fish hatchery, where she got in her little blue Subaru Outback and followed him back to the cabin.

They stayed on.

To sit on the porch as the night fell, to wander into the forest hand in hand, laughing together under the tall trees, sharing stories of their families, of their lives up till now.

They spent a lot of time naked upstairs in the bed under the eaves. And downstairs, on the couch, in the big brown chair, wherever and whenever the mood struck—which was often.

And every time was better than the time before.

On New Year's Eve, they didn't bother to get dressed the whole day. They made love and napped all wrapped up together and toasted in the New Year with whiskey from a dusty bottle Matthias pulled from the back of a cupboard.

And then, all of a sudden, totally out of nowhere, it was New Year's Day.

She didn't want to go.

But that was the thing. She *had* to go. She had her life to cobble back together. She had her promise to herself, to *get* a life, a full and happy life, on her own.

And they had a deal. It was a good deal. Christmas together.

And nothing more.

He helped her carry her stuff to her Outback. It only took one trip. And then he held her in his arms and kissed her, a kiss so right and so consuming, she had no idea how she was going to make herself get in the car and drive away.

He cradled her face in those big, wonderful hands and his blue eyes held hers. "God. I don't want to say goodbye."

Her eyes burned with tears she wouldn't let fall. "Me neither." It came out in a ragged whisper because her throat had clutched with sadness and yearning for what would never be. She lifted up and brushed her lips to his once more, breathing in the evergreen scent of him. *I will never forget*, she promised in her heart. Overhead, a bird cried, a long, keening sound. "Goodbye, Matthias."

"Wait." He pulled something from his jacket pocket. "Give me your hand."

She held it out. He took it, turned it palm up and set a key there, then gently folded her fingers over the cool metal. She looked up at him, confused, searching his face that she'd already come to love—just a little. "What's this?"

"A key to the cabin."

"But—"

He stopped her with a finger against her lips. "So here's my offer. I work flexible hours, fill in for everyone else all year long. Except at Christmas, when they give me first crack at the schedule. I'll be right here, same time, next year, from the twenty-third till New Year's Day. Alone. If you maybe find that you wouldn't mind spending another Christmas with me, just the two of us, just for Christmastime, well then, you have the key."

"Matthias, I—"

"Uh-uh." He brushed his thumb across her mouth. She felt that slight touch all the way down to the core of her. His eyes were oceans she wanted to drown in, an endless sky in which she longed to take flight. "Don't decide now. A lot can happen in a year."

She threw her arms around him and buried her face against his shoulder. "I miss you already."

He said her name, low. Rough. They held each other hard and tight.

And then, by silent mutual agreement, they both let go and staggered back from each other. She stuck the key in her pocket to join the wooden porcupine he'd given her.

He pulled open her door for her and shut it once she was behind the wheel, tapping the door in a final salute.

She watched him turn and go up the steps.

That was as much as she could take of him walking away. She started the engine, put it in Drive and headed for Portland.

Chapter Six

Matt, the following June...

It was Friday night at Beach Street Brews in Valentine Bay. The music was too loud and the acoustics were terrible. The barnlike brew pub was wall-to-wall bodies, everybody laughing, shouting, meeting up, partying down.

Matt nursed a beer and wished he hadn't come.

Jerry Davidson, his friend since first grade, pulled out the chair next to him and dropped into it. "C'mon!" Jerry shouted in Matt's ear. "I met a girl. She's at the bar. And she's got a good-looking friend."

Matt raised his mug and took another sip. "Have fun."

The band crashed through the final bars of Kongos' "Come with Me Now." The applause was thunderous. "We'll be back," growled the front man into the mic.

When the clapping faded down, Matt enjoyed the relative silence.

Until Jerry leaned close and started talking again. "It's that girl, isn't it? The one from the cabin? You're thinking about her, aren't you?"

He was, yeah. But no way was he getting into that with Jerry. He never should have told his friend about Sabra. Sabra was *his*. A perfect memory to treasure. He didn't have a whole hell of a lot of those and Jerry needed to quit telling him to move on.

"Leave it alone," Matt said. "I told you. It's

not going anywhere. It was great and now it's over." *Unless she shows up again at Christmas.*

God. He hoped she would.

But too much could happen in the space of a year. Sabra was hot and smart, kind and funny and easy to talk to. In spite of her vow to stay single for years, by Christmas, some lucky bastard would coax her into giving love another try. Matt hated that guy with a pure, cold fury. Whoever the hell he might turn out to be.

At least once a week he almost convinced himself it would be okay to look her up online. He never did it, though. And he *wouldn't* do it. They had an agreement and he would keep the promise he'd made to her.

Jerry clapped him on the shoulder. "You need to relax and have a good time."

"Jer. How many years you been giving me that advice?"

"Hmm." Jerry stroked his short, thick ginger beard. "Several."

"Do I ever listen?"

"Before last Christmas, you used to. Now and then."

"I'm not in the mood." Matt tipped his head toward the bar. "And a pretty woman is waiting on you."

Jerry glanced up to give his latest conquest a quick wave. "You're insane not to come with me."

"Go."

Jerry gave it up and headed back to the bar.

Matt nursed his beer and wished it was Christmas.

Sabra, that September...

"More wine?" Iris held up the excellent bottle of Oregon pinot noir. At Sabra's nod, her friend refilled her glass.

It was girl's night in at Iris and Peyton's apartment in downtown Portland—just the three of them. Sabra could safely afford to indulge in the wine. Back in January, she'd rented a one-bedroom in this same building, so home was two flights of stairs or a very short elevator ride away.

Peyton, her caramel-colored hair piled in a messy bun on the top of her head, turned from the stir-fry she was cooking and asked Sabra, "So can I tell him to give you a call?"

"He's a hottie." Iris did a little cha-cha-cha with her shoulders, her hair, which she wore in natural corkscrew curls, bouncing in time with the movement. "And no drama, which we all love."

He was Jack Kellan, the new sous chef at Delia Mae's, where they all worked.

"Jack is a great guy," Sabra said, thinking of Matthias as she did every time her friends got after her to get out and mix it up—and no, she hadn't told anyone about what had happened at Christmas. It was her secret pleasure, having known him, everything they'd shared. Often, she found herself wondering where he was and what he might be doing right now.

But no, she wasn't getting attached, wasn't pining for her Christmas lover. Uh-uh. No way.

Iris scoffed. "Could you *be* any less enthusiastic?" Iris had that Tyra-Banks-meets-Wendy-Williams thing going on. All power, smarts and sass. Nobody messed with Iris. "This swearing-off-men thing? Sabra, honey, it's not a good look on you."

Totally out of nowhere, emotion made her eyes burn and her throat clutch. "I'm just not ready yet, you know?"

Iris set down the bottle of pinot and peered

at her more closely across the kitchen island. "Something's really got you bothered. What?"

"Come on, now." Peyton turned off the heat under the stir-fry and she and Iris converged on either side of Sabra. "You'll feel better if you talk about it."

"Is it your dad?" Iris ventured gently.

Sabra drooped on her stool as her friends shared a knowing look.

"It's her dad," confirmed Peyton.

Sabra had been up to the farm a few days before. As usual, she'd come home earlier than planned. "He's just worse every time I see him. He's thinner, more withdrawn than ever. I want to be there for him, but he won't talk about it, about Mom. It's like there's a brick wall between him and the rest of the world. Nobody gets in, not even me."

"Oh, honey…" Iris grabbed her in a hug and Peyton wrapped her arms around both of them.

Sabra leaned her head on Iris's shoulder. "I keep telling myself he'll get better. But the years keep going by and he only seems sadder and further away, like he's slowly fading down to nothing. It scares me, it does. And I don't know what to do about it."

Her friends rubbed her back and hugged her some more. They offered a number of suggestions and Sabra thanked them and promised to try to get her dad to maybe join a men's group or see a therapist. They all agreed that Adam Bond had been a prisoner of his grief for much too long.

There was more wine and Peyton's delicious stir-fry. Iris talked about the guy she'd just broken up with and Peyton was all dewy-eyed over the new man in her life. By midnight, Sabra was feeling the wine. She looked from one dear friend's face to the other—and she just couldn't hold back any longer.

"Ahem. There is something else I keep meaning to tell you guys…"

"Hmm," said Peyton thoughtfully. She and Iris exchanged yet another speaking glance.

Iris nodded. "We knew it."

"Spill," commanded Peyton.

Sabra set down her empty glass. "It's like this. Last Christmas, when I was supposedly snowed in at the farm?"

"Supposedly?" Iris scowled. "Meaning you weren't?"

Sabra busted to it. "I wasn't at the farm and I wasn't alone."

"A man," said Peyton. It wasn't a question.

"That's right. I stopped off on the way back here to Portland for a hike—you know, trying to get out of my own head a little. I started walking and it started raining. I took shelter at this empty cabin. And then the owner arrived…"

They listened without interrupting as she

told them about Matthias, about her Christmas at the cabin, about pretty much all of it, including how he'd given her a key as she was leaving, just in case she might want to spend another Christmas with him.

Iris screeched in delight and Peyton declared, "Now, that's what I'm talking about. James the jerk? He couldn't keep you down. He goes back to the baby mama he'd forgotten to mention and what do you do? Head out for some hot, sexy times with a hermit in the forest."

Sabra whacked her friend lightly with the back of her hand. "Matthias is not a hermit. He has a real job and a big family in Valentine Bay."

"He just hides out alone in an isolated cabin for Christmas," teased her friend.

"Not last Christmas, he didn't," Sabra said smugly. Her friends high-fived her for that and she added more seriously, "He's had some rough times in his life and he likes to get off by himself now and then, that's all."

Peyton scolded, "You took way too long to tell us, you know. It's been months and months. It's almost the holidays all over again."

"Yeah, well. Sorry. But I wasn't going to tell *anyone*, ever. Overall, it was a beautiful time, the *best* time. And after I got back to Portland, well, I kind of thought of it as our secret, Matthias's and mine."

"We get it," said Iris.

"But we're still glad you finally told us," Peyton chimed in.

Iris nodded. "It's a yummy story, you and the cabin guy."

Peyton was watching Sabra a little too closely. "Look at me," she commanded. When Sabra met her gaze, Peyton shook her head. "I knew it. You're in love with him, aren't you?"

No way. "Nope. Not a chance. I'm immune to love now, not going there again."

"Of course you will go there again," argued Iris.

"Well, if I do, it won't be for years. And anyway, how could I possibly be in love with him? I knew him for ten days."

"You should just call him," Iris advised.

"I told you. I don't have his number and I'm not tracking him down online because getting in touch wasn't part of the deal—and yeah, I still have the key to the cabin. But that doesn't mean I'll be meeting him in December."

Her friends didn't argue with her, but she saw the speaking glance that passed between them.

Matt, December 1...

The three-legged Siberian husky Matt had named Zoya followed him into his bedroom.

He'd found her hobbling along the highway on his way home from Warrenton, four months ago now. No collar, no tags. He'd coaxed her to come to him and, after some hesitation, she did, so he'd driven her to the shelter here in Valentine Bay. They'd checked for an ID chip. She didn't have one.

Two weeks later, he stopped by the shelter to see if her former owner had come for her.

Hadn't happened. No one had adopted her, either.

The vet who helped out at the shelter said the husky was just full-grown, two or three years old and in excellent health. Her left front leg had been amputated, probably while she was still a puppy. She was well trained, happy natured and responded to all the basic commands.

Matt had done some research and then had a long talk with the vet about caring for a tripod dog. By then, he was pretty much all in on Zoya.

He brought her home. It was a little like having a kid, a well-behaved kid who wanted to please. He took her to doggy day care every workday, where she got lots of attention and pack time with other dogs.

Him. With a dog.

Matt wasn't sure what exactly had gotten into him to take her. But when she looked at him with those unearthly blue eyes, well, he could relate, that was all. She needed a human of her own. And he'd been available. Plus, it was time he stepped up, made a commitment to another creature even if he wasn't ready to give love with a woman any kind of a chance.

His four sisters all adored her. He'd taken her to a couple of family gatherings. The first time he showed up with Zoya, the oldest of his sisters, Aislinn, had pulled him aside...

"I have to ask." Aislinn gazed at him piercingly. "A *Siberian* husky?"

He understood her implication. "Yeah, well.

I probably would have adopted her anyway, but it seemed more than right, you know? I only have to hear the word *Siberian* and I think of Finn. It's good to be reminded, to never forget."

Ais's dark eyes welled with moisture. "Nobody blames you."

"I know. But I do blame myself because I am culpable. If I'd behaved differently that day, Finn might be here with us now."

"Mom blamed *herself*."

"Yeah, well, there's plenty of blame to go around."

"Matt. Mom gave you permission to go off on your own—and then she told Finn that it was fine if he went with you."

"It is what it is, that's all. Now, stop looking so sad and let's hug it out."

With a cry, Ais threw herself at him. He

wrapped his arms around her and held on tight, feeling grateful.

For his family, who had never given up on him no matter how messed up he got. For Zoya, who seemed more than happy to have him as her human.

And also for Sabra Bond, who had managed to show him in the short ten days he'd spent with her that maybe someday he might be capable of making a good life with the right woman, of starting a family of his own.

"How 'bout a walk, girl?"

Zoya gave an eager little whine and dropped to her haunches.

Matt crouched to give her a good scratch around the ruff. "All right, then. Let me get changed and we're on it."

He took off his uniform, pausing when he stepped out of his pants for a look at the crescent-shaped scar from that little run-in with his own ax last Christmas. It was no more than a thin, curved line now. Sabra had patched him up good as new. The older scar on his other leg was much worse, with explosions of white scar tissue and a trench-like indentation in the flesh along the inside of his shin. There were pins and bolts in there holding everything together. He'd almost lost that leg below the knee.

But almost only counts in horseshoes. And now, that leg worked fine, except for some occasional stiffness and intermittent pain, especially in cold weather when it could ache like a sonofagun.

In his socks and boxer briefs, he grabbed a red Sharpie from a cup on the dresser and went to the closet. Sticking the Sharpie between his teeth to free both hands, he hung up his uniform. Once that was done, he shoved everything to the side, the hangers rattling as they slid along the rod.

The calendar was waiting, tacked to the wall. It was a large, themed calendar he'd found at Freddy's—Wild and Scenic Oregon. He'd bought it for what could only be called sentimental reasons. Bought it because he couldn't stop thinking of Sabra.

Sappy or not, marking off the days till Christmas had made him feel closer to a woman he hadn't seen in months, a woman he'd actually known for one week and three days.

For November, the calendar offered a spectacular photo of the Three Sisters, a trio of volcanic peaks in Oregon's section of the Cascade Range. Below the Three Sisters, he'd x-ed out each of November's days in red.

Lifting the calendar off the tack, he turned it to December and a picture of Fort Clatsop in the snow. He hooked it back in place and pulled the top off the Sharpie. With a lot more satisfaction than the simple action should have inspired, he x-ed off December 1.

Already, there was a big red circle around the ten days from December 23 to New Year's.

Satisfaction turned to real excitement.

Only twenty-one days to go.

December 23, three years ago...

It was late afternoon when Matt turned onto the dirt road that would take him to the cabin.

He had a fine-looking tree roped to the roof rack and the back seat packed with food, Christmas presents, and the usual duffel bags of clothes and gear. The weather was milder this year, real Western Oregon weather— cloudy with a constant threat of rain, no snow in the forecast.

Zoya, in her crate, had the rear of the vehicle. He would have loved having her in the passenger seat next to him, but with only one front leg, a sudden lurch or a fast stop could too easily send her pitching to the floor.

He was nervous, crazy nervous—nervous enough to be embarrassed at himself. The eager drumming of his pulse only got more so as he neared the clearing. He came around the second-to-last turn where he'd seen the lights in the windows the year before, hope rising...

Nothing.

Maybe she was waiting on the front porch.

He took the final turn.

Nobody there.

The nervous jitters fled. Now his whole body felt heavy, weighed down at the center with disappointment, as he pulled to a stop in front of the porch.

She hadn't come—not yet, anyway.

And he really had no right to expect that she would. He'd offered. It was her move.

And maybe she'd simply decided that one Christmas alone with him had been plenty. She was smart and beautiful and so much fun to be with. She'd probably found someone else.

He had to face the likelihood that she wouldn't show.

That she'd moved on.

That he would never see her face again.

He could accept that. He would *have* to accept it, his own crazy longing and the carefully marked calendar in his bedroom closet aside.

Reality was a bitch sometimes and that wasn't news.

He got out, opened the hatch in back, let Zoya out of her crate and helped her down to the ground. "Come on, girl. Let's get everything inside."

* * *

An hour later, he had the fire going, the Jeep unpacked, the groceries put away, and Zoya all set with food and water by her open crate. The tree stood proud in the stand by the window, not far from the front door. It was bigger and thicker than last year, filling the cabin with its Christmassy evergreen scent. A box of presents waited beside it. He'd even carried all his gear upstairs.

The disappointment?

Worse by the minute.

But he wasn't going to let it get him down. "Okay, sweetheart," he said to his dog. "I'm going to bring down the decorations and we'll get this party started."

Zoya made a happy sound, followed by a wide yawn. She rolled over and offered her belly to scratch, her pink tongue lolling out

the side of her mouth, making her look adorably eager and also slightly demented.

"Goofy girl." He crouched to give her some
attention. But before he got all the way down,
she rolled back over and sat up, ears perking.

And then he heard the sound he'd been
yearning for: tires crunching gravel.

His heart suddenly booming like it would
beat its way right out of his chest, he straightened. Out the front windows, he watched as
the familiar blue Subaru Outback pulled to
a stop.

Chapter Seven

By a supreme effort of will, Matt managed not to race out there, throw open her car door, drag her into his arms, toss her over his shoulder and carry her straight up the stairs.

His tread measured, with Zoya at his heels, he crossed the cabin floor, opened the door and stepped out into the cold, gray afternoon. The dog whined, a worried sort of sound. She liked people, but new ones made her nervous—at first, anyway.

"Sit."

Zoya dropped to her haunches on the porch, still whining, tail twitching.

Sabra. Just the sight of her filled him with more powerful emotions than he knew how to name.

She got out of the car.

Hot damn, she looked amazing in tight jeans, lace-up boots and a big sweater printed with Christmas trees.

"You cut your hair." It came to just below her chin now.

Standing there by her car, looking shy and so damn pretty, she reached up and fiddled with her bangs. Her gorgeous face was flushed, her deep brown eyes even bigger than he remembered. "I don't know. I just wanted a change."

"It looks good on you."

A secret smile flashed across those lips he couldn't wait to taste again. She gave a tiny nod in acknowledgment of the compliment, her gaze shifting to Zoya. "You have a dog?"

Zoya knew when someone was talking about her. She quivered harder and whined hopefully. "More like she has me. I found her on the highway, dropped her off at the animal shelter—and then couldn't stop thinking about her."

Sabra laughed. God, what a beautiful sound. "Can't resist a pretty stray, huh? Such gorgeous blue eyes she's got. What's her name?"

"Zoya."

"I like it. Is it Polish, or…?"

"Russian." He gave a shrug. "She's a Siberian husky. It seemed to fit."

"Is it okay if I introduce myself?"

"Sure."

She clicked her tongue and called the dog.

When Zoya hesitated, he encouraged her. "It's all right, girl. Go." And she went, tail wagging, hopping down the steps to greet the woman Matt couldn't wait to kiss.

He followed the husky down to the ground and gave the woman and the dog a minute to get to know each other. By the time Sabra rose from giving Zoya the attention she craved, he couldn't wait any longer.

He caught her arm, heat zapping through him just to have his hand on her, even with the thick sweater keeping him from getting skin to skin. "Hey."

"Hey."

"I'm really glad to see you." It came out in a low growl.

She giggled, the cutest, happiest little sound. "Prove it."

"Excellent suggestion." He pulled her in close, wrapping both arms around her. And then he kissed her.

Zap. Like an electric charge flashing from

her lips to his. Her mouth tasted better than he remembered, which couldn't be possible. Could it? He framed her face with his two hands and kissed her some more.

It wasn't enough. He needed her inside, up the stairs, out of her clothes…

She let out a little cry as he broke the kiss—but only to get one arm beneath her knees. With the other at her back, he scooped her high against his chest.

"I'm taking you inside," he announced.

"Yes," she replied, right before he crashed his mouth down on hers again.

He groaned in pure happiness, breathing in the scent of her, so fresh, with a hint of oranges, probably from her shampoo. Whatever. She smelled amazing. She smelled like everything he'd been longing for, everything he'd feared he would never touch or smell or taste again.

Kissing her as he went, he strode up the steps, across the porch and on inside, pausing only to wait for Zoya to come in after them before kicking the door shut with his foot.

Sabra broke the kiss to look around, her hands clasped behind his neck, fingers stroking his nape like she couldn't get enough of the feel of his skin. "The tree looks so good, even better than last year. And it smells like heaven." She pressed her nose against his throat. "It smells like you…"

"We'll decorate it," he said gruffly when she tipped her head away enough to meet his eyes again. "Later." He nuzzled her cool, velvety cheek, brushed a couple of quick kisses across her lips.

"You're so handsome. So big. So…" She laughed, a carefree sort of sound. "I am *so* glad to see you."

"Likewise, only double that—wait. Make that quintuple."

She stroked a hand at his temple, combing her fingers back into his hair. "I have stuff to bring in."

"Later." Zoya stood on her three legs looking up at them, tipping her head from side to side, not quite sure what the hell was going on. "Stay," he commanded, as he headed for the stairs.

"Your leg seems better."

"Good as new."

"I can walk, you know," she chided.

"Yeah. But I don't know if I can let go of you." He took her mouth again. Desire sparked and sizzled through his veins. Already, he was so hard it hurt.

"I've missed you, too," she whispered into the kiss.

"Not as much as I've missed you." He took

the stairs two at a time and carried her straight to the bed, setting her down on it, grabbing the hem of her big sweater. "I like this sweater."

"Thanks."

"Let's get it off you." He pulled it up.

She raised her arms and he took it away, tossing it in the general direction of a nearby chair. She dropped back on her hands. He drank in the sight of her, in her skinny jeans and a lacy red bra, the kind a woman wears when a man might be likely to see it, to take it off her.

"So pretty." He eased his index finger between one silky strap and her skin and rubbed it up and down, from the slight swell of her breast to her shoulder and back again. Happiness filled him, bright and hot, to go with the pleasure-pain of his powerful desire. He bent closer, right over her, planting both fists on the mattress to either side of her. "I have an idea."

Her eyes went wide. "Yeah?"

"Let's get *everything* off you. Let's do that now."

A slow smile was her answer.

He dropped to his knees at her feet and untied her boots, pulling them off and her snowflake-patterned socks right after them. She shoved down her jeans. He dragged them free and tossed them aside.

In her red bra and a lacy little thong to match, she reached for him, pulling him up beside her—and then slipping over the edge of the bed to kneel and get to work on *his* boots.

He helped her, bending down and untying one as she untied the other. They paused only long enough to share a quick, rough kiss and in no time, he was out of his boots and socks. The rest of his clothes followed quickly. He ripped them off as she climbed back on the bed and sat on folded knees.

Resting her long-fingered hands on her smooth thighs, breathing fast, she stared at him through eyes gone black with longing. Reaching behind her, she started to unclasp her bra.

"No." He bent across the bed to still her arms. "Let me do that." *Or not.* He allowed himself a slow smile. "And on second thought, this bra and that thong might be too pretty to take off."

She caught the corner of her mouth with her teeth, her eyes promising him everything as she brought her hands to rest on her thighs again.

He took her by the wrists and tugged. She knelt up. Scooping an arm around her, he hauled her to the edge of the bed and tight against him. "It's been too long," he muttered, dipping his head to kiss that sweet spot where her neck met her shoulder.

The scent of her filled him—oranges, flowers, that beautiful sweetness, the essence of her, going musky now with her arousal.

He kissed her, another deep one, running his tongue over hers, gliding it against the ridges of her pretty teeth.

So many perfect places to put his mouth.

He got to work on that, leaving her lips with some reluctance, but consoling himself with the taste of her skin, licking the clean, gorgeous line of her jaw, moving on down to bite the tight flesh over her collarbone. She moaned when he did that and tried to pull him closer. He resisted. He had plans of his own.

Slowly, he lowered her bra straps with his teeth, using a finger to ease the lacy cups of the bra under her breasts so he could kiss those pretty, puckered nipples. She looked so amazing, with her face flushed, her eyes enormous, pure black, hazy with need, and her breasts overflowing the cups of that red bra.

He backed up again. When she moaned in protest and grabbed for him, he commanded, "Stretch out your legs."

She scooted back to the middle of the bed and stuck her feet out in front of her. "Like this?"

"Just like that." He grabbed her ankles and pulled. With a surprised laugh, she braced her hands behind her as he hauled her to the edge of the bed again.

"Lie back," he instructed as he went to his knees, pushing her smooth thighs apart to get in close and tight.

As he kissed her through the lace of that teeny-tiny thong, she moaned and fisted her fingers in his hair. "Matthias, please!" He glanced up at her sharp cry. "It's been a year. Come up here, right now. Come here to me."

He couldn't argue—didn't want to argue. He needed to be joined with her. He needed that right now.

And the gorgeous, soaking-wet thong? In the way.

He hooked his fingers in at both sides of it, pulled it down and tossed it halfway across the room. She undid the pretty bra and dropped it to the floor as he rose to yank open the bedside drawer. He had the condom out and on in record time.

"Come down here." She grabbed hold of his arm and pulled him on top of her, opening for him, wrapping those strong legs around him. Holding him hard and tight with one arm, she wriggled the other between them, took him in hand and guided him right to where they both wanted him.

"At last," she whispered, pushing her beautiful body up hard against him, wrapping her legs around him even tighter than before.

He was wild for her, too. With a surge of his hips, he was deep inside.

She cried out as he filled her.

"Too fast?" He groaned the words. "Did I hurt you?"

"No way." She grabbed on with both hands, yanking him in even tighter. "Oh, I have missed you."

"Missed you, too," he echoed. "So much…"

And he lost himself in her. There was only Sabra, the feel of her beautiful body around him, taking him deep.

They rolled and she was above him. That was so right, just what he needed—until they were rolling again, sharing a laugh that turned into rough moans as they arrived on their sides, facing each other, her leg thrown across him, pulling him so close. She urged him on with her eager cries.

He didn't want it to end. She pulled him on top again. Somehow, he held out through her first climax, gritting his teeth a little, groaning at the splendid agony of it as she pulsed around him. It was like nothing else, ever—to feel her giving way, giving it up, losing herself in his arms.

When she went limp beneath him, he sank into her, kissing her, stroking her tangled hair, waiting for the moment when she began to move again.

He didn't have to wait long.

Hooking her legs around him once more, she surged up against him. With a deep groan, he joined her in the rhythm she set as she chased her second finish all the way to the top and over into free fall.

That time, he gave it up, too, driving deep within her as the pleasure rolled through him, rocketing down his spine, opening him up and sending him soaring.

Leaving him breathless, stunned—and deeply happy in a way he couldn't remember ever being before.

By the time Matthias let her out of bed an hour later, Sabra was starving.

Luckily, she'd brought fresh sourdough bread and a variety of sandwich fixings. They carried the food in from the Subaru and she made sandwiches while he unloaded the rest of her things.

Once they'd filled their growling bellies, he put on the Christmas tunes and they decorated the tree—working together this year, which meant the whole process was a whole lot more fun and took half the time it had the year before.

She'd brought ornaments. "You need at least one new ornament every year," she explained.

"I do?" He got that look guys get when women tell them how it ought to be, that *Huh*? kind of look that said women's logic really didn't compute.

"I brought three." She grabbed her pack from its hook on the far side of the door and pulled them out, each in its own small box. "Open them."

He obeyed, taking them from the boxes and hanging them on the tree. They included a porcupine carved from a pinecone, a crystal snowflake—and a blown glass pickle.

"Each has an important sentimental meaning…" She let the words trail off significantly.

He was up for the game. "Let me guess. The porcupine because I gave you one last year. And the snowflake to remind me that being snowed in can be the best time a guy ever had—he just needs to be snowed in with you."

She nodded approvingly. "What about the pickle?"

He turned to study the ornament in question, which he'd hung on a high branch. It was nubby and dark green, dusted with glitter, twinkling in the light. "It's a very handsome pickle, I have to say."

"You're stalling."

"Hmm." He pretended to be deep in thought over the possible significance of a pickle.

She scoffed at him. "You haven't got a clue."

"Wait." He put up a hand. "It's all coming back to me now."

"Yeah, right."

"Didn't I read somewhere that you hide a pickle ornament on the tree and the kid who finds it gets something special? Also, I think I remember hearing that pickle ornaments bring good luck."

"You're actually smirking," she accused.

"Me? No way. I never smirk."

"You knew all along."

He caught her hand and pulled her in close. "Do you think I'll get lucky?" He kissed her. "Never mind. I already have."

"Oh, yeah," she answered softly. "Pickle or no pickle, from now until New Year's, I'm your sure thing."

Later, they had hot chocolate on the front porch, with Zoya stretched out at their feet and gnawing enthusiastically on a rawhide bone.

Sabra had barely emptied her mug and set it down on the porch beside her chair when Matthias held out his hand to her.

The second she laid her fingers in his, he

was pulling her up and out of the chair, over onto his lap.

Things got steamy fast. In no time, she was topless, with her pants undone.

She loved every minute of it, out there in the cold December night, with the hottest man she'd ever met to keep her toasty warm.

The next morning, he snuck down the stairs while she was still drowsing. When she followed the smell of fresh coffee down to the main floor, he didn't say a word until she'd savored that first cup.

"I have a Christmas Eve request," she said over breakfast.

He rose from his chair to bend close and kiss her, a kiss that tasted of coffee and cinnamon rolls and the promise of more kisses to come. "Anything. Name it."

"I want to finish the hike to the falls that I started last year."

He sank back to his chair. "It's rough going. Lots of brush and then several stretches over heavily logged country, where it's nothing but dirt and giant tree stumps, most of them out of the ground, gnarly with huge roots."

She gave him her sweetest smile. "You said 'anything.' And I still want to go."

They set out half an hour later.

Matthias kept Zoya on a leash most of the way. They wound through barren stretches of rough, logged terrain, eventually entering the forest again, where the trail was so completely overgrown, it grew difficult to make out the path.

They bushwhacked their way through it. At one point, Sabra turned to look back for no particular reason—and saw snowcapped Mt. Rainier in the distance. She got out her phone and snapped a picture of it.

They went on to the top of the falls. It wasn't much to look at. The trees grew close and bushy, obscuring the view. They drank from their water bottles and he poured some into a collapsible bowl for Zoya.

"It's beautiful from below." He pointed into the steep canyon. "I mean, if you're up for beating your way down through the bushes."

"Yes!" She said it with feeling, to bolster her own flagging enthusiasm for the task. The overcast sky seemed to be getting darker. "No rain in the forecast, right?"

He gave her his smug look. "Or so all the weather services have predicted."

"We should get back, huh?"

He pretended to consider her question. "I thought you wanted to get a good view of the falls."

She leaned his way and bumped him with her shoulder. "That sounds like a challenge."

He gave a lazy shrug. "It's no problem if you think it's too much for you."

She popped the plug back into her water bottle. "That does it. We are going down."

And down they went.

Zoya was amazing, effortlessly balanced on only three legs. She bounced along through the underbrush, never flagging. Sabra and Matthias had a little more difficulty, but they kept after it—and were rewarded at the bottom by the gorgeous sight of the tumbling white water from down below.

"Worth it?" he asked.

"Definitely." She got a bunch of pictures on her phone.

"Come here." He hooked his giant arm around her waist and hauled her close, claiming her lips in a long, deliciously dizzying kiss. She got lost in that kiss—lost in *him*, in Matthias, in the miracle of this thing between them that was still so compelling after a whole year apart.

Twice in her life, she'd almost said *I do*, but

she'd never felt anything like this before. She loved just being with him, making love for hours, laughing together, sharing the most basic, simple pleasures, the two of them and Zoya, in a one-room cabin.

Or out in the wild at the foot of a waterfall.

A drop of rain plopped on her forehead. Then another, then a whole bunch of them.

It was like someone up there had turned on a faucet. The sky just opened wide and the water poured down.

They both tipped their faces up to it, laughing.

"Why am I not the least bit surprised?" she asked.

He kissed her again, quick and hard, as the water ran down her face and trickled between their fused lips.

"Come on." He pulled up her hood and snapped the closure at her throat. "Let's find shelter. We can wait out the worst of it."

"What shelter?" She scoffed at him. "I haven't seen any shelter."

"Follow me." He pulled up his own hood. "Zoya, heel." He set off, the dog looping immediately into position on his left side. "Good girl." He pulled a treat from his pocket. Zoya took it from his hand as he started back up the hillside. Sabra fell in behind them.

When they got to the trail, it was still coming down, every bit as thick and hard as the day they'd met. They set off back the way they'd come. She had waterproof gear this time, so most of her stayed dry. It could have been worse.

About a mile or so later, Matthias veered from the path they'd taken originally. The brush grew denser and the rain came down harder, if that was even possible.

"Did you say there would be shelter?" she asked hopefully from behind him.

Just as the question escaped her lips, a shelf-like rock formation came into view ahead. She spotted the darkened space between the stones. He ducked into the shadows, Zoya right behind him.

Sabra followed. It was a shallow depression in the rock, not quite a cave, but deep enough to get them out of the deluge.

"Get comfortable." He slid off his pack and sat with his back to the inner wall. Zoya shook herself, sending muddy water flying, and then flopped down beside him as Sabra set her pack with his. "It could be a while." He reached up a hand to her.

She took it, dropping to his other side, pulling on his hand so that she could settle his arm across her shoulders. "Cozy."

"Ignore the muddy dog smell."

She pushed back her hood and sniffed the air. "Heaven." And it kind of was, just to be with him. A world apart, only the two of them and Zoya and the roar of the rain outside their rocky shelter. She asked, "What's your deepest fear?"

"Getting serious, are we?" He pressed his cold lips to the wet hair at her temple.

"Too grim? Don't answer."

"No, it's good. I can go there. A desk job would be pretty terrifying."

"You're right." She leaned her head on his shoulder. "All that sitting. Very scary."

"I like to keep moving."

"Me, too."

"What are *you* afraid of?" he asked.

She didn't even need to think about it. "That I'll never be able to make myself go back and live at our farm."

He waited until she looked up into his waiting eyes. "It's that bad?"

"Yeah. Because it was so good once. I have

too many beautiful memories there, you know? The farm was always my future, always what I wanted to do with my life. And now it's just a sad place to me. I go for a visit, and all I want is to leave again."

He tipped up her chin with the back of his hand. "How's your dad doing?"

She gazed up into those deep blue eyes and felt *seen*, somehow. Cherished. Protected. Completely accepted. "He's thin, my dad. It's like he's slowly disappearing. I need to spend more time with him. But I can't bear to be there. Still, I *need* to be there. I told him at Thanksgiving that I would move home, work the farm with him, the way we always planned. I said I wanted to spend more time with him."

"You sound doubtful."

"I guess he noticed that, too. He said that he was doing fine and he knew that coming home wasn't going to work for me. He said that I had my own life and I should do what *I* wanted."

"He's a good guy, huh?"

"My dad? The best—just, you know, sad. The lights are on but he's not really home." She laid her head on his shoulder again. They watched the rain together.

She must have dozed off, because she suddenly became aware that the rain had subsided to a light drizzle. Zoya's tags jingled as she gave herself a scratch.

And suddenly, Sabra wanted to get up, move on. "Let's hit the trail, huh?"

"Sure."

They shouldered their packs and set out again.

Matt really wouldn't have minded at all if this holiday season never came to an end. It was so easy and natural with Sabra. They could talk or not talk. Tell each other painful truths, or hike for an hour without a word spoken. Didn't matter. It was all good.

Back at the cabin, they gave Zoya a bath.

Then they rinsed the mud out of the tub and took a long bath together. That led to some good times on the sofa and then later upstairs.

They came down to eat and to play Scrabble naked. She beat the pants off him—or she would've, if he'd had pants on.

By midnight, she was yawning. She went on upstairs alone. He put his clothes back on. Then he and Zoya, some nice blocks of basswood and his Swiss Army knife spent a couple of quality hours out on the porch.

He climbed the stairs to the loft smiling.

When he slid under the covers with her, she shivered and complained that his feet were freezing. But when he pulled her close and wrapped himself around her, she gave a happy sigh and went right back to sleep.

Christmas morning zipped past in a haze of holiday tunes, kisses and laughter.

Matt had left the gifts from his family at home to open later and they gave each other simple things, silly things. He'd carved her another porcupine, a bigger one, for a doorstop. She had two gifts for him: a giant coffee mug with the woodsman's coat of arms, which included crossed axes and a sustainable forestry slogan; and a grenade-size wilderness survival kit that contained everything from safety pins to fish hooks and lines, water bags, candles and a knife.

The afternoon was clear and they went for another hike.

On the twenty-sixth, they drove down the coast to the pretty town of Manzanita and had dinner at a great seafood place there. He'd almost suggested they try a restaurant he liked in Astoria, but then decided against it. They had an agreement, after all, to keep their real lives separate. She'd told him last year that her farm was near Svensen, which was technically in Astoria. He kind of thought it might be pushing things, to take her too close to home.

And he *wasn't* pushing, he kept reminding himself. She'd said she wasn't ready for anything more than the great time they were having. And he wasn't ready for a relationship, either.

Or he hadn't been.

Until a certain fine brunette broke into his cabin and made him start thinking impossible things. Like how well they fit together.

Like how maybe he *was* ready to talk about trying again with a woman—with *her*.

He kept a damn calendar in his closet, didn't he? A paper one. Who even used paper calendars anymore?

Just lovesick guys like him, schmaltzy guys who had to literally count the days, mark them off with big red x's, until he could finally see her again.

But how to have the taking-it-to-the-next-level conversation?

He felt like he could say anything to her—except for the thing he most wanted to say.

Sabra, I want more with you. More than Christmas and New Year's. I want the rest of the winter.

And the spring and the summer. And the fall?

I want that, too.

I want it all, Sabra. I want it all with you.

But the days zipped by and he said nothing.

And then the more he thought about it, well, maybe he really wasn't ready. If he was ready, he would open his mouth and say so, now wouldn't he?

* * *

The only problem with this Christmastime as far as Sabra was concerned?

It was all flying by too fast.

Phone numbers, she kept thinking.

Maybe they could just do that, exchange phone numbers. Really, they were so close now, a deep sort of closeness, sometimes easy. Sometimes deliciously intense.

She couldn't bear to just drive away and not see him until next year—or maybe never, if he found someone else while they were apart. If he...

Well, who knew what might happen in the space of twelve months? They hadn't even talked about whether or not they would meet up again next year.

She needed his phone number. She needed to be able to call him and text him and send him pictures. Of her. In a pink lace bra and an itty-bitty thong.

Seriously, the great sex aside, it was going to be tough for her, when she left him this year. She felt so close to him. It would be like ripping off a body part to say goodbye.

But then, that was her problem, wasn't it?

She got so attached. There was no in-between with her. She fell for a guy and started picking out the china patterns.

This, with Matthias, was supposed to be different. It was supposed to be a way to have it all with this amazing man, but in a Christmas-sized package. With a date-certain goodbye.

Exchanging numbers was a slippery slope and she was not going down it. She was enjoying every minute with him.

And then, on the first of January, she was letting go.

All of a sudden, it was New Year's Eve.

Matt and Sabra stayed in bed, as they had the year before, only getting up for food and bathroom breaks and to take a shower to-gether—and twice, to take Zoya out for a lit-tle exercise.

Matt willed the hours to pass slowly—which only made them whiz by all the faster.

Sabra dropped off to sleep at a little after midnight. He lay there beside her, watching her beautiful face, wanting to wake her up just to have her big eyes to look into, just to whisper with her, have her touch him, have her truly *with* him for every moment he could steal.

Man, he was gone on her.

It was powerful, what he felt for her. Too powerful, maybe.

Dangerous to him, even. To his hard-earned equilibrium.

He'd lived through a boatload of loss and guilt. The guilt over Finn had almost destroyed him before he was even old enough to legally order a beer.

Sometimes he still dreamed about it, about that moment when he turned around in the snowy, silent Siberian wilderness, and his annoying eight-year-old brother wasn't there.

He'd been angry that day—for the whole, endless trip up till then—angry at his parents, at the crap that they put him through, with their damn love of traveling, of seeing the world. That year, it was Russia. They saw Moscow and Saint Petersburg—and of course, they had to visit the Siberian wilderness.

Daniel, the oldest, had somehow gotten out of that trip. That made Matt the main babysitter of his seven younger siblings.

It had happened on a day trip from Irkutsk. They'd stopped for lunch somewhere snowy and endless; off in the distance, a stand of tall, bare-looking trees. Matt just had to get away.

He decided on a walk across the flat snow-covered land, out into the tall trees. He told his parents he was going.

"Alone," he said, scowling.

His mom had waved a hand. "Don't be such a grouch, Matt. Have your walk. We'll keep the other kids here."

He set out.

And Finn, always adventurous, never one to do what he was told to do, had tagged along behind him.

Matt ordered him to go back to the others.

Finn just insisted, *Mom said I could come with you*, and kept following. And then he started chattering, about how he thought the huskies that pulled their sled were so cool, with their weird, bright blue eyes, how he wanted a husky, and he was going to ask Mom for one.

Matt still remembered turning on him, glaring. *"Just shut up, will you, Finnegan? Just. Please. Stop. Talking."*

Finn had stared up at him, wide-eyed. Hurt. Proud. And now silent.

He never said another word.

Five minutes later, Matt turned around again and Finn was gone.

That really was his fault, losing Finn. The guilt that ate at him from the inside was guilt he had earned with his own harsh words, with the ensuing silence that he'd let go on too long.

His parents died two years later, on the first trip they'd taken since Finn disappeared. That trip was just the two of them, Marie and George Bravo, a little getaway to Thailand, to try to recapture the magic they found in traveling after the tragic loss of their youngest son. They'd checked in to the resort just in time for the arrival of the tsunami that killed them.

To Matt, the Thailand getaway had seemed

a direct result of his losing Finn in Russia. He'd been sure in his guilty heart that his parents would never have been in Thailand if not for him.

After his parents died, Matt was constantly in trouble. And if you could drink it, snort it or smoke it, Matt was up for it in high school and during those two years at CCC. The only good thing in his life then had been Christy, his girl.

He told Christy everything, all of his many sins. She loved him and forgave him and made him feel better. Until she grew tired of waiting for him to come home from the other side of the world, dumped him and married someone else.

As for Mark and Nelson, well, at least he didn't actively blame himself for their deaths in Iraq. All he'd done in that case was to survive—which had brought its own kind of guilt.

Survivor guilt, he'd learned through living it, was just as bad as the guilt you felt for losing your own brother. It had taken a whole lot of counseling to get on with his life after Iraq.

But he *had* gotten on with it. He was doing all right now, with a good life and work that he loved. He'd even taken a big step and gotten himself a dog.

And now there was Sabra. And he couldn't help wanting more than Christmas with her.

Just ask for her number. How dangerous can that be?

Damn dangerous, you long-gone fool.

When a man finally finds a certain equilibrium in his life, he's reluctant to rock the boat—even for a chance to take things further with someone like Sabra.

Morning came way too soon. He made her coffee and she drank it in the usual shared silence.

Then he dragged her upstairs again, where they made love once more.

They came down and had breakfast, went outside and sat out on the porch for a while.

And then, around noon, Sabra said she had to get going.

Matt helped her load her stuff into the Subaru. It took no time at all, the minutes zipping by when all he wanted was to grab onto them, make them stand still.

Too soon, they were saying their goodbyes, just like last year, but with Zoya beside them.

Sabra knelt to give his dog a last hug.

When she rose again, she said, "I don't have the words." She gazed up at him through those deep brown eyes that he knew he'd be seeing in his dreams all year long. "It's been pretty much perfect and I hate to go."

Don't, then. Stay. "I hate to *see* you go."

She eased her hand into a pocket and came out with the key.

No way. He caught her wrist and wrapped her fingers tight around it. "Next year. Same time. I'll be here. I hope you will, too."

"Matthias." Those big eyes were even brighter with the shine of barely held-back tears. "Oh, I will miss you…"

Stay.

But he didn't say it. Instead, he reached out and took her by the shoulders, pulling her in close, burying his nose against her hair, which smelled of sunshine and oranges. She wrapped her arms around him, too. He never wanted to let her go.

But it had to be done.

Slowly, she lifted her head. He watched a tear get away from her. It gleamed as it slid down her cheek. Bending close, he pressed his mouth to the salty wetness.

She turned her head just enough so their lips could meet. He gathered her even tighter in his arms, claiming her mouth, tasting her deeply.

The kiss went on for a very long time. He wished it might last forever, that some miracle might happen to make it so she wouldn't go.

But she hadn't said a word about taking it further—and neither had he.

Her arms loosened around him. He made himself take his hands off her and reached for the door handle, pulling it wide.

She got in and he shut it.

With a last wave through the glass of the window, she started the engine.

He stepped back. Zoya gave a whine.

"Sit," he commanded.

The husky dropped to her haunches beside him. He watched Sabra go, not turning for the porch steps until the blue Subaru disappeared around the first bend in the twisting dirt road.

Chapter Eight

The following May...

Sabra stood by the empty hospital bed her father didn't need anymore. She held a plastic bag full of clothes and other personal belongings that Adam Bond wouldn't ever wear again.

Really, there was nothing more to do here at Peaceful Rest Hospice Care. She should go.

But still, she just stood there, her dad's last words to her whispering through her head. *Don't cry, sweetheart. I love you and I hate to leave you, but I'm ready to go. You see, it's not really cancer. It's just my broken heart...*

"There you are." Peyton stood in the open door to the hallway.

Iris, who stood behind her, asked, "Have you got everything?"

Words had somehow deserted her. Sabra hard-swallowed a pointless sob and held up the bag of useless clothing.

"Oh, honey," said Peyton, and came for her, Iris right behind her.

They put their arms around her, Iris on one side and Peyton on the other. She let herself lean on them and felt a deep gratitude that they were there with her.

"Come on," whispered Iris, giving her shoulders a comforting squeeze. "It's time to go."

That June...

At Berry Bog Farm, the office was the large extra room at the rear of the house, between the kitchen and the laundry room, just off the narrow hallway that opened onto a screened-in porch.

Sabra sat at the old oak desk that had been her father's and his father's before him. She scrolled through the spreadsheet showing income and expenses as she waited for Nils Wilson, her father's longtime friend and top farmhand.

The back door to the screen porch gave a little screech as it opened.

She called out, "In the office, Nils!" and listened to the sound of his footfalls on the wide-plank floor as he approached.

He appeared in the doorway to the back hall, tall and skinny as ever, with a long face to match the rest of him. Deep grooves had etched themselves on either side of his mouth and across his high, narrow forehead. "Hey, pumpkin." He'd always called her pumpkin, for as long as she could remember.

She got up and went to him for a hug. He enfolded her in his long arms. She breathed in the smell of cut grass and dirt that always seemed to cling to him, a scent she found infinitely comforting, a scent to soothe her troubled soul. She asked after his wife of thirty-two years. "How's Marjorie?"

"About the same." Twenty-four years ago, when Sabra was still toddling around in diapers, Nils and Marjorie had put up a manufactured home across the front yard from the farmhouse. Marjorie worked wherever she was needed. She raised goats and chickens and she ran the farm's fresh flower business. She sold gorgeous bunches of them at local markets and also to several florist shops in the area. "She runs me ragged." Nils put on a long-suffering look.

Sabra smiled at that. "And you wouldn't have it any other way."

"Humph," said Nils, meaning yes. He liked to play it grumpy sometimes, but everyone knew how much he loved his wife.

"I missed her this morning when I drove in." Sabra gestured toward the two guest chairs opposite the desk. Nils followed her over there and they sat down.

"You know how she is," said Nils. "Up with the roosters, ready to work."

"I know. I'll catch her this evening."

"Come for dinner?"

"I'll be there."

He reached across the short distance between them to put his wrinkled, work-roughened hand over hers. "How're you holdin' up?"

Her throat ached, suddenly, the ache of tears. She gulped them down. "All right."

He shook his head. "Pumpkin, you were his shining light."

She sniffed and sat up straighter. "No. Mom was that. But he was a good dad. The best." *And I should have been here for him.*

Nils gave her hand a squeeze before pulling back. "So. We're gonna talk business now, is that it?"

"Yes, we are."

"Good. When are you coming home to stay?"

That lump in her throat? It was bigger than ever. "Well, I, um…"

Nils got the message. "You're not coming home." He said it flatly, his disappointment clear.

"I just, well, I hope you and Marjorie will stay on."

"Of course we will."

"We'll change our arrangement. I will drive up every couple of weeks, to keep on top of things. But you'll be running the place. Both you and Marjorie will be getting more money."

"Pumpkin, I got no doubt you will be fair with us. That's not the question. It's about you."

"Nils, I—"

"No. Now, you hear me out. You are a Bond, a farmer to the core. You were born to run Berry Bog Farm. I just want you to think on it. You belong here with us. Won't you come home at last?"

"I'm just, well, I'm not ready to do that and I don't know when I will be ready."

What she didn't tell him was that she was considering putting the farm up for sale. She *would* tell him, of course, as soon as she'd made up her mind.

Right now, though?

She felt she ought to sell, that she would never be able to come back and live here, that just showing up every few weeks to go over the books and handle any necessary business was almost more than she could bear. There were far too many memories here, from happy through bittersweet all the way to devastating.

So yeah. She ought to sell. If she did, she would see to it that Nils and Marjorie were provided for. But no matter how much she settled on them, they wouldn't be happy if she sold the place. The farm was their home.

And really, she couldn't stand the thought of that, either, of letting the land that was her heritage go.

Which left her in a bleak limbo of grief and indecision.

Later, in the evening, after dinner with the Wilsons, she trudged upstairs to her dad's room and tackled packing up his things. As she cleaned out his closet, her thoughts turned to Matthias. She missed him. She ached to have a long talk with him, to feel his muscled arms around her. Life would be so much more bearable if she could have him near.

She paused, her head in the closet, one of her dad's plaid jackets in her hands—a Pendleton, red and black. Adam Bond had always been a sucker for a nice Pendleton. Shirts, jackets, coats, you name it. He had a lot of them. They were excellent quality. People knew he liked them and gave them to him for Christmas and his birthday.

A sob stuck in her throat because he would never wear his Pendletons again.

Backing out of the closet with the jacket in her hand, she sank to the edge of the bed, putting her palm down flat on the wedding ring quilt her mom had made before Sabra was even a twinkle in her dad's eye.

Idly, she traced the circular stitching in the quilt, thinking of Matthias—his blue, blue eyes, his beautiful, reluctant smile. The way he held her, sometimes hard and tight, like he wanted to absorb her body into his. And sometimes so tenderly, with a deep, true sort of care.

Really, it wouldn't be difficult at all to track him down. He worked for the Department of Fish and Wildlife locally and he had a big family in Valentine Bay.

Would he be angry with her for breaking their rules?

Or would he hold out his arms to her and gather her close? Would he say how happy he was that she'd come to find him? Would he promise her that eventually this grayness would pass, that things would get better and life would make sense again?

She laughed out loud to the empty room, a hard, unhappy sound.

Because she was being sloppy and sentimental. She wasn't going to contact him. She and

Matthias had what they had. It was tenuous and magical and only for Christmas.

No way would she ruin it by trying to make it more.

That July...

Matt had two remaining relatives on his mother's side of the family—Great-Uncle Percy Valentine, who'd given him the cabin, and Percy's sister, Great-Aunt Daffodil Valentine.

In their eighties, the never-married brother and sister lived at Valentine House on the edge of Valentine City Park. Matt found his great-aunt and uncle charming and eccentric, sharp-witted and no-nonsense. Daffy and Percy came to all the big family gatherings. But Matt made it a point to drop by and see them at home now and then, too.

He always brought takeout when he came.

This time, Daffy had requested "Bacon cheeseburgers with the works, young man."

Matt knew how to take an order and arrived bearing grease-spotted white bags from a Valentine Bay landmark, Raeleen's Roadside Grill. He'd brought the cheeseburgers, fries, onion rings and milkshakes—chocolate for him and Daffy, vanilla for Uncle Percy.

Letha March, who'd been cooking and cleaning at Valentine House for as long as Matt could remember, answered the door and ushered him and Zoya into the formal parlor, which contained too much antique furniture, an ugly floral-pattered rug, and his great-aunt and uncle.

"You got Raeleen's!" Daffy clapped her wrinkled hands in delight. "You always were my favorite great-nephew."

"Aunt Daffy, I know you say that to all of us."

Daffy patted his cheek and smiled up at him

fondly as Percy bent to greet Zoya. Letha got out the TV trays so they could chow down right there in the parlor the way they always did.

As they ate, Uncle Percy reported on his progress with the search for Finn. Percy, who often referred to himself as "the family sleuth," had been in charge of the search from the beginning. He worked with private investigators, a series of them. Each PI would find out what he or she could and turn in a report. And then Percy would hire someone else to try again. Each investigator got the benefit of the information his predecessors had uncovered. For all the years of searching, they hadn't found much.

But Percy would never give up. And he and Matt had agreed that when, for whatever reason, Percy could no longer run the search, Matt would step up.

"So there you have it," Percy concluded. "As usual, it's not a lot."

Matt thanked him and they made encouraging noises at each other in order not to get too discouraged. No matter how hopeless it seemed sometimes, the worst thing would be to give up and stop looking.

Daffy slipped Zoya a French fry. "Now tell us what is happening in your life, Matthias." She and Percy always called him by his full name.

Same as Sabra did.

Sabra.

He'd been thinking of her constantly. He wanted more time with her, wanted to take it beyond the cabin, make it real between them. They could go slow. She was in Portland, after all. They would have to make some effort to be together.

But he was willing. He wanted to be with her. Whatever it took.

"What is that faraway look in your eye?" asked Uncle Percy.

Matt shocked the hell out of himself by telling them the truth. "I've met someone. Her name is Sabra Bond. Born and raised on a farm near Astoria. Now she manages a restaurant in Portland. She has dark hair and big brown eyes and she's smart and funny and tough and beautiful. I'm crazy about her."

He told them how and when he'd met her and about the two Christmases they'd spent together at the cabin. He even explained about the agreement—just the two of them, just for Christmas, no contact otherwise.

"But you want more," said Aunt Daffy.

"I do, yeah."

"It does my old heart good," said Uncle

Percy, "to see you coming back from all you've been through."

Daffy gave a slow nod. "You are truly healing, Matthias, and that is a beautiful thing to see."

Uncle Percy reached over and clapped a hand on his arm. "Finding yourself, that's what you're doing. Didn't I tell you that you would?"

"Yes, you did."

"We're so happy for you," cried Daffy.

"I just… I'm not sure how to try for more with her, not sure how to ask her, not sure what to say."

"Just speak from your heart," advised Daffy. "The specific words will come to you, as long as you show your true self and tell her clearly what you want."

Percy added, "Be honest and forthright and it will all work out."

Later that night, at home, Matt considered

taking Percy's advice to heart immediately. How hard could it be to find her, really? On-line searches aside, there were only so many farms on the outskirts of Astoria.

But then, well, no.

Stalking the woman wasn't part of their deal.

Being patient wouldn't kill him. He would wait for Christmas and pray she showed up this year, too.

Matt marked another X on his calendar, bringing him one day closer to seeing her again.

That September...

"Come on, man." Jerry tipped his head toward the dark-haired woman three tables over. "She's a knockout and she likes you. What are you saving it for, I'd just like to know?" It was yet another Friday night at Beach Street

Brews and as always, Jerry was after him to hook up with someone.

Matt wondered why he'd come. "Cut it out, Jer. Let me enjoy my beer." Matt needed that beer. He also needed not to be hassled while drinking it.

A week before, his brother Daniel's wife Lillie had given birth to twins, Jake and Frannie. The twins were fine, but two days after the birth, Lillie had died from complications mostly due to lupus. It was a tough time in the Bravo family.

And the last thing Matt needed right now was a night with a stranger.

Jerry poured himself another glass from the pitcher on the table between them. "This is getting ridiculous. I've gotta meet your holiday hookup, see what's so special you're willing to go all year without—"

"Drop it, Jerry." Matt turned and looked his

aggravating friend squarely in the eye. "Just let it go."

"I don't get it. That's all I'm sayin'."

"Yeah, well. You've said it. Repeatedly. I heard you. Stop."

"It's not healthy to—"

"That does it." Matt shoved back his chair. "I'm outta here."

"Aw, c'mon, man. Don't get mad."

"You have fun, Jerry." Matt threw some bills on the table.

Jerry looked kind of crestfallen. "Listen. I'm sorry. I've got a big mouth, I know. I should try to keep a lid on it."

"Yeah, you should—and you're forgiven."

"Great. C'mon, stay."

He clapped his friend on the shoulder. "Gotta go."

"So…maybe *I* should make a move on her?" Jerry gave the dark-haired woman a wave.

Matt just shook his head and made for the door.

Three months left until Christmas at the cabin. Losing Lillie really had him thinking that life flew by way too fast, that everything could change when you least expected it and a man needed to grab what he wanted and hold on tight.

This year, if Sabra showed up, he was not letting her go without asking for more.

December 23, two years ago…

She was already there!

Matt saw the lights gleaming from the cabin windows at the same turn where he'd spotted them two years before. His heart seemed to leap upward in his chest and lodge squarely in his throat. His pulse raced, gladness burning along every nerve in his body as he rounded the next turn and the turn after that.

The front door swung open as he rolled into the yard and pulled to a stop behind the Subaru.

Sabra emerged dressed in a long black sweater and leggings printed with reindeer and snowflakes, knee-high boots on her feet. Her hair was longer this time, the dark curls loose on her shoulders. He couldn't wait to get his hands in them.

Shoving the car into Park, he turned off the engine, threw the door wide and jumped out to catch her as she hurled herself into his outstretched arms.

"At last," they whispered in unison.

And then he was kissing her, breathing in her sweet, incomparable scent, going deep, hard and hungry. She laughed as he angled his mouth the other way and she jumped up, lifting those fine legs and wrapping them good and tight around him, her arms twined behind his neck.

He was halfway up the steps, devouring her mouth as he went, before she broke their liplock and started to speak. "I'm so—"

"Get back here." He cradled her head, holding her still so he could claim those beautiful lips again.

Before he crashed into her that time, she got a single word out. "Zoya?"

He groaned, gentled his hold and pressed his forehead to hers. "See what you do to me? I almost forgot my own dog."

She took his face between her hands and offered eagerly, "One more kiss?"

He gave it to her, long and deep, turning as he kissed her, heading back down the steps. She dropped her feet to the ground at the back of the vehicle. He let her go reluctantly and opened the hatch. Zoya rose in her crate, stretching and yawning. "Sorry, girl," he muttered. Behind him, he heard Sabra chuckle. "C'mon out." He opened the crate and helped the husky down to the ground.

"Zoya! It's so good to see you." Sabra knelt to greet her, scratching her ruff, giving her long strokes down her back as Zoya whined and wriggled with happiness. "I've missed you so much…"

Matt waited impatiently for her to finish her reunion with his dog. When she finally rose, he reached for her again.

She danced away, laughing, her gaze on the tree tied to the roof rack. "I swear, you found a thicker tree than last year. So gorgeous…"

"Just beautiful," he agreed. He wasn't referring to the tree. Catching her elbow, he pulled her close again. "So then. Where were we?"

Those dark eyes held a teasing light. "We should bring it in, put it in water and—"

With a growl, he covered her sweet mouth with his, taking her by the waist and then lifting her. She got the hint, surrendering her mouth to him as she wrapped her legs and arms around him again.

He carried her up the steps and in the door without stopping that time, counting on Zoya to stick close behind. As soon as they cleared the threshold, Sabra stuck out a hand and shoved the door shut.

Reluctantly, he lifted his mouth from hers, noting that not only had she gotten the fire going, she'd set out water for Zoya. The dog was already lapping it up.

"Oh, I cannot believe you're actually here." Her smile could light up the darkest corner of the blackest night.

"It's been too long," he grumbled.

"Oh, yes it has." She caught his lower lip between her pretty teeth and bit down lightly, sending heat and need flaring even higher within him.

"That does it," he muttered. "We're going upstairs."

"Yes," she replied, suddenly earnest. "*Now*, Matthias. Please."

He told Zoya to stay and started walking, carrying her up there, kissing her the whole way.

At the bed, she clung to him. He started undressing her anyway, pulling her long sweater up and away, not even pausing to give her lacy purple bra the attention it deserved, just unhooking it, ripping the straps down and whipping it off her, revealing those beautiful high pink-tipped breasts. "Everything. Off," he commanded, peeling her legs from around him, setting her down on the mattress.

She didn't argue. He stripped and she stripped. In a short chain of heated seconds, they were both naked. He went down to the bed with her, grabbing for her, gathering her close.

This was no time to play.

It had been way too long and he couldn't wait. Lucky for him, she seemed to feel the same.

"Hurry," she egged him on. "I have missed you so much..."

He touched the heart of her: soaking wet, so ready.

"Yes," she begged him. "Please. I want you now."

With a groan, he stuck out a hand for the bedside drawer.

She curled her fingers tightly around him, bringing a rough moan of pure need from him as she held his aching length in place. He rolled the condom halfway on and she took over, snugging it all the way down.

That did it. He was not waiting for one second longer.

Taking her by the shoulders, he rolled her under him, easing his thigh between hers and coming into her with a single deep thrust.

She moaned his name and wrapped her legs and arms around him, pulling him in so tight against her, as though she couldn't bear to leave an inch of empty space between her body and his.

They moved together, hard and fast. There was nothing but the feel of her, the taste of her mouth, the scent of her silky hair tangling around him, the heat of her claiming him, taking him down.

He gave himself up to it—to her, to this magic between them, to the longing that never left him in the whole year without her.

"Yes!" she cried, and then crooned his

name, "Matthias, missed you. Missed you so much…"

Just barely, he held himself back from the brink, waiting for her, drawing it out into sweet, endless agony.

And then, at last, she cried out and he felt her pulsing around him. Through a monumental effort of will, he stayed with her as she came apart in his arms. Finally, with a shout of pure triumph, he gave in and let his finish take him down.

So tightly, he held her, never wanting to let go.

But when he finally loosened his hold on her, she gave a gentle push to his shoulders. He took the hint and braced up on his arms to grin down at her.

But his grin didn't last.

She met his gaze, her eyes haunted looking

in her flushed face. Her soft mouth trembled. "Oh, Matthias."

"What? Sabra, what's the matter?"

Her face crumpled and she burst into tears.

Chapter Nine

"Sabra—sweetheart, talk to me. Come on, what is it?" Matthias was staring down at her, golden eyebrows drawn together, clearly stunned at this out-of-nowhere crying jag.

The tears poured from her, blurring her vision. "Sorry. So sorry. I can't… I don't…" Apparently, complete sentences were not available to her right now. She sniffled loudly and swiped at her nose.

"Stay right there," he instructed, easing his

body off hers. She squinted through her blurry eyes, trying to contain her sobs as he removed the condom and tied it off. The tears wouldn't stop falling.

Miserable, she turned away from him. Curling herself in a ball, she tried to get control of herself, but for some reason, that only made the tears come faster.

The bed shifted as he rose.

A minute later, he touched her shoulder, the gentlest, kindest sort of touch. "Hey. Here you go…"

With a watery little sob, she rolled back to face him. "Just ignore me. That's what you should do. Just go on downstairs and—"

"I'm going nowhere. Here. Take these." He handed her a couple of tissues.

"Oh, Matthias." She swiped at her nose and her cheeks. "This, um, isn't about you. I hope you know that. I'm so glad to see you. So glad to be with you. But this…" She gestured with the tissues at the whole of herself. "I don't know why I'm doing this. I don't know… what's the matter with me, to be such a big crybaby right now." She sniffled and stared up at him, *willing* him to understand, though she'd said nothing coherent so far, nothing to help him figure out what was bothering her. "I don't know what I'm saying, even. Because, what *am* I saying? I have no idea."

"It's okay."

"No, it is not."

"Well, I can see that. But I mean, between me and you, everything is okay. I'm right here and whatever you need, I'll do whatever it takes to make sure you get it." He got back on the bed with her. "Now, come here." He took her shoulders gently. She scrambled into his lap like an overgrown child and buried her face against his broad, warm chest. "You're safe," he soothed. "I'm right here." He stroked her hair, petted her shoulder, rubbed his big hand up and down her back.

She huddled against him, relishing the comfort he offered, matching her breaths to his in order to calm herself, endlessly grateful to have his steady strength to cling to.

For several minutes, neither of them spoke. He held her and she was held by him. Finally, she looked up to find his eyes waiting.

"What is it?" he asked. "Talk to me."

She sniffled and wiped more tears away. "My dad died."

His forehead scrunched up. "Oh, Sabra." He ran his hand down her hair, brushed a kiss against her still-wet cheek. "When?"

"In the spring. He, um, it was cancer, non-Hodgkin's lymphoma. He didn't get treatment. Not for years, I found out later. And by the time he did, it was too late. He, well, he wanted to die. He told me so, right there at the end—not that he *had* to tell me. I knew. He never got over my mom's death. He just, well, he didn't want to be in this world without her."

Matthias pulled her close again. She felt his warm breath brush the crown of her head. "I'm so sorry…"

She wiped her nose with the wadded-up tissues. "I should feel better about it. I mean, he got what he wanted, right?"

He kissed her temple. "That doesn't mean you can't miss him and want him back with you."

"He was ready. He said so."

"But *you* weren't ready to lose him."

She tipped her face up to meet his clear blue eyes again. "You're right. I wasn't ready. I also wasn't *there* when he needed me. He would always say he was fine and he understood that I needed to get out, make my own way, move to Portland, all that." Another hard sob escaped her. She dabbed her eyes and shook her head. "I should have tried harder, should have kept after him, gotten him to a doctor sooner. When he said he was all right, I just accepted it, took his word for it. And now, well, he's gone and I've got more regrets than I can name. I can't bear to sell the farm, but I couldn't stand to live there, either. It's like I'm being torn in different directions and I can't make up my mind, can't decide which way to go."

"So don't decide."

She blinked at him, surprised. *"Don't* decide?"

"Do you have someone you trust taking care of the farm?"

"Yeah, but—"

"If you don't *have* to decide right now, don't. Wait."

"Wait for…?"

"Until you're ready."

"But I'm a mess. How am I supposed to know when I'm ready?"

He looked at her so tenderly, not smiling, very serious. But there was a smile lurking in his eyes, a smile that reassured her, that seemed to promise everything would somehow work out right in the end. "The question is, do you think you're ready to decide about the farm right now?"

"God, no."

"Well, there you go. Take it from someone who's had a whole hell of a lot of therapy. When you're grieving, it's not a good time to have to make big choices. Sometimes life doesn't cooperate and a choice *has* to be made anyway. Then you do the best you can and hope it all works out. But you just said you don't have to decide right this minute.

So don't. Procrastination isn't always a bad thing."

She turned the idea over in her mind. "Don't decide…"

"Not until you either *have* to decide, or you're sure of what you want."

What he said made a lot of sense. "Okay then. I will seriously consider procrastination." She giggled at the absurdity of it—and realized she felt better. She really did. Sometimes a girl just needed a long, ugly cry and some excellent advice.

She snuggled in close, enjoying his body heat. For a little while, they simply sat there in the middle of the rumpled bed, holding each other.

"What about you?" she asked softly. "Any big changes in your life since last Christmas?"

He told her of his sister-in-law, who'd died in early September after giving birth to twins.

"Her name was Lillie. She was only a year older than me, but still, she was kind of a second mother to all of us after our parents died, so losing her is a little like losing our mom all over again."

She lifted up enough to kiss his cheek. "That's so sad."

"Yeah. We all miss her. And my brother Daniel, her husband, has always been one of those too-serious kind of guys. Since Lillie died, I don't think anyone has seen Daniel crack a smile."

"Give him time."

"Hey. What else can we do?"

"Life is just so *hard* sometimes..." She tucked her head beneath his chin and he idly stroked her hair.

Downstairs, she heard Zoya's claws tapping the wood floor. The husky gave a hopeful little whine.

Sabra stirred. "We should get moving. Your dog is lonely and your Jeep is not going to unload itself."

The next day, Christmas Eve, they decorated the tree and Matt took her out to dinner at that seafood place in Manzanita. When they got back to the cabin, they sat out on the porch until after midnight, laughing together, holding hands between their separate chairs until he coaxed her over onto his lap. It started snowing.

"It's beautiful," she said as they watched the delicate flakes drifting down.

"And the best kind, too," he agreed.

She chuckled and leaned her head against his shoulder. "Yeah. The kind that doesn't stick."

By Christmas morning, the snow had turned to rain.

All Christmas day and the day after, Matt tried to find the right moment to talk about the future. That moment hadn't come yet, though. But he was waiting for it, certain he would know when the time was right.

It was a bittersweet sort of Christmas. Sabra had lost her dad and Lillie was gone from the Bravo family much too soon. Still, Matt was hopeful. He felt close to Sabra—closer than ever, really.

Every hour with her was a gift, fleeting, gone too soon. But exactly what he needed, nonetheless. She was everything he wanted, everything he'd almost given up hope of having in his life.

Like last year, they went hiking together. He loved that she enjoyed a good, sweaty hike, that she didn't mind slogging through the rain on rough, overgrown terrain for the simple satisfaction of doing it, of catching sight of a hawk high in the sky or a misty waterfall from deep in some forgotten ravine.

He wanted her, *all* of her. He wanted her exclusively and forever. They were meant to be together. He just knew it was time for them to make it *more*.

Too bad that the right moment to ask for her phone number never quite seemed to come.

And the days? They were going by much too fast.

Five days after Christmas, they got up nice and early. Matt made the coffee and was silent while Sabra had her first cup. They ate breakfast and took Zoya for a walk.

Back in the cabin, Sabra grabbed his hand and led him upstairs. They peeled off their clothes and climbed into bed. The lovemaking was slow and lazy and so good. It only got really intense toward the end.

They'd just fallen away from each other,

laughing and panting, when Zoya started whining downstairs.

Sabra sat up, listening. "Is that a car outside?"

Zoya barked then, three warning barks in succession.

By then, Matt was out of the bed and pulling on his jeans. "I'll see what's up." He zipped up his pants and ran down the stairs barefoot, buttoning up his flannel shirt as he went.

The knock on the door came just as he reached the main floor. From the foot of the stairs, he could see out the front windows.

Parked behind his Jeep and Sabra's Outback was a Silverado 4x4 with the Oregon State Police logo on the door and State Trooper printed over the front wheel.

Matt instructed Zoya to sit and opened the door. "Jerry," he said wearily.

Jerry grinned. "Hey, buddy. Hope I didn't

interrupt anything. I was in the area and I thought, why not stop in and say hi?"

As if he didn't know what his old friend was up to. "You should call first."

Jerry got that busted look. "Yeah, well I…" He swiped off his hat and leaned around him. "Hey!"

"Hello," Sabra said as she came up beside him wearing the sweater and jeans he'd taken off her a half hour before.

Matt introduced them.

Sabra seemed okay with Jerry dropping in. Matt had mentioned his friend to her in passing more than once. She was aware that Jerry and Matt had known each other most of their lives.

Really, it shouldn't be a big deal, but it pissed Matt off that Jerry had dropped in without checking first, mostly because of what Jer had said that night in September, about how he *had* to meet Sabra, had to see what was so special about her.

"You want some coffee?" Matt asked grudgingly, causing Sabra to shoot him a questioning frown. She'd guessed from his tone that he wasn't happy.

Jerry gave a forced laugh. He knew he was out of bounds. "Coffee would be great."

They had coffee and some Christmas cookies Sabra had brought. They made casual conversation. Jerry said the tree was beautiful and too bad the snow hadn't stuck at least through Christmas day and blah-blah-blah. At least he was charming and friendly with Sabra.

"I'll walk you out," Matt said when Jerry got up to go.

"Uh, sure." Jerry said how great it was to have met Sabra and she made the same noises back at him.

"I'll be right back," Matt promised.

She gave him a nod, and he followed Jerry out to his patrol truck.

"Okay, what?" mumbled Jerry when they reached the driver's door. "Just say it."

"You got a phone. I got a phone. Why didn't you call first?"

Jerry put his hat back on. "I wanted to meet her, okay? I was afraid you'd say no." Matt just looked at him, dead-on. Jerry stuck his hands in his pockets. "All right, yeah. I should have called. And I'm sorry." He looked kind of sad.

And why was it always damn-near impossible to stay pissed off at Jerry? "I told you the situation. As of now, friends and family don't enter into what I have with her."

"I get it. My bad."

"Don't pull anything like that again."

"Never." Jerry looked appropriately chastised—but then he slanted Matt a hopeful glance. "She's hot and I like her—and you said 'as of now'? You're planning to take it to the next level, then? Because really, man, I only want you to get whatever makes you happy."

Matt kind of wanted to grab his friend and hug him. But he needed to be sure that Jerry got the message. "Stay out of it, Jer."

"Yeah. I hear you, man. Loud and clear." He climbed in behind the wheel. "Happy New Year, buddy."

"Happy New Year."

"I liked your friend," Sabra said when Matt got back inside the cabin.

"Everybody likes Jer. He told me he thinks you're hot."

One side of her gorgeous mouth quirked up in a reluctant smile. "I'm flattered—I think." She caught the corner of her lip between her teeth, hesitating.

"Go ahead and say it."

"Well, is everything okay with you and him? You seemed kind of annoyed with him."

His heart rate accelerated and his skin felt too hot. He wanted to tell her, right then, how he felt, what he longed for with her.

Was this it, the right time, finally? He stared at her unforgettable face that he missed the whole year long and ached to go for it, this very minute, to finally ask her to consider giving him more than the holidays.

Staring at her, though? It never was enough. He reached out and slipped his hand under the silky fall of her hair. Curling his rough fingers around her smooth nape, he pulled her nice and close. She tipped up her chin and he claimed a kiss.

And when he lifted his head, somehow the moment to ask the big question had passed.

"Well?" she prompted.

"I wasn't happy that he just dropped in without calling, that's all."

"Isn't that kind of what friends do?"

"Sure, mostly. But Jerry *knows*."

"About us, you mean?"

He nodded. "I told him that I'm crazy about you."

She smiled then, a full-out smile. "You did?"

He wished she would smile at him like that every day. Every day, all year round. "Absolutely. Jerry knows we just have Christmastime, that it's just you and me, away from our real lives."

"So, if he'd asked first, you would have told him to stay away?"

"I don't know. I would've asked you. Found out how you felt about his coming by. We would have decided together." And now he *had* to know. "How *do* you feel about it?"

She was biting the corner of her lip again. "I guess you're right. It's supposed to be just us, just for the holidays. Inviting our friends in isn't part of the deal."

Ouch. That wasn't at all what he'd hoped she might say.

Tell her. Ask her. Do it now.

But he hesitated a moment too long.

And she asked, "When you went out to the truck with him, did you make it up with him?"

He let the main issue go to answer her question. "I did. I can never stay mad at Jerry."

"Well, good." She stepped in close again, put her slim hands on his chest and slid them up to link around his neck. "What do you say we take Zoya for a nice long walk?" At their feet, the husky whined her approval of that suggestion. "The weather's just right for it."

He grunted. "Yeah, cloudy with a chance of rain."

"Welcome to Oregon." She kissed him, after which they put on their boots and took the dog outside.

* * *

The rest of that day was gone in an instant and the night that followed raced by even faster.

All of a sudden, it was New Year's Eve. Time for naked Scrabble and naked Clue—naked everything, really. Matt and Sabra only got dressed to take the dog outside.

At midnight, they toasted in the New Year with a nice a bottle of champagne courtesy of Sabra. Upstairs, they made love again. And again after that.

She drifted off to sleep around two in the morning.

Matt stayed awake, planning what he would say before she left tomorrow, trying to think of just the right words that would make her agree they were ready for more than the holidays together.

By noon New Year's Day, he still hadn't said anything. Apparently, he was a complete wimp when it came to asking for what he wanted the most.

At a little after one in the afternoon, she said she had to get her stuff together and get on the road. He helped her load up the Outback, as he had the year before and the year before that.

And then, way too soon, long before he was ready, they were standing by her driver's door and she was saying goodbye. She knelt and made a fuss over Zoya, and then she rose and moved in close, sliding her hands up over his chest slowly, the way she loved to do, hooking them at the back of his neck.

"I hate to leave." She kissed him, a quick brush of those soft lips across his.

He stared down at her, aching inside. She was getting away from him and if she left now without him opening his damn mouth and saying what he needed to say, he would have to break their agreement and track her down in Portland. Either that, or he wouldn't set eyes on her for another damn year—maybe never if something happened and one of them didn't show up next December.

He'd been waiting for the right moment, the right moment that somehow never came. And now here they were and she was going and it was *this* moment.

Or never.

"Matthias?" Her sleek eyebrows drew together in concern. "What's the matter? What's happened?"

He clasped her shoulders—too hard, enough that she winced. "Sorry." He forced himself to loosen his grip. "I…" The words tried to stick in his throat. He pushed them out. "Sabra, I want more."

She stared up at him, her eyes growing wider. "Um, you want…?" He waited. But that was it. That was all she got out.

He tried again. "*This*, you and me for Christmas. It's beautiful. Perfect. Except that it's not enough for me, not anymore. I want to be with you, spend time with you when it's not Christmas. I want to see you in February, in June and in the fall. I want, well, I was thinking we could just start with phone numbers, maybe? Just exchange numbers and then try getting together soon, see how it goes."

She only stared up at him, eyes enormous in her suddenly pale face.

Was this going all wrong?

He kind of thought it might be.

Should he back off?

Probably.

But he'd been such a damn coward for the last ten days. He needed to go for it. Now that he'd finally opened his mouth and said what he wanted, he needed to take it all the way. "Sabra, I—"

She silenced him by putting up her hand between them, pressing her fingers to his lips. "Oh, I just, well, I thought we understood each other, we agreed that we—"

"Stop." He caught her wrist. "Let me finish."

With a shaky sigh, she nodded, carefully pulling free of his grip, stepping back from him—one step. Two.

He got on with it, because no way could he wait another year to tell her what was in his heart. "I'm in love with you, Sabra." A tiny cry escaped her, but she caught herself, pressing her hand to her mouth, swallowing down whatever she might have said next. He barreled on. "I want the rest of my life with you. But I know I'm never going to get it if I don't tell you how much I want you, want *us*, you and me, together. In the real world. I want to meet your friends and introduce you to my family. I want to show you my hometown and get the tour of your farm. I don't want to push you, I—"

"That's not fair." She spoke in an angry whisper.

He blinked down at her. "Excuse me?"

"You *are* pushing me, Matthias. You're asking me for things that I don't know how to give."

Okay, now. That kind of bugged him. That made him mad. He said, way too quietly, "How am I going to have a prayer of getting more from you if I don't ask for it?"

"Well, it's just that we have an agreement. And yet, all of a sudden, you're all about forever."

"Sabra, it's been two years—two years and three Christmases. That is hardly 'all of a sudden.'"

Her soft mouth twisted. "You know what I mean."

"Uh, no. I guess I don't."

"Well, um, last year, for instance?"

"What about it?"

"Last year, I was kind of thinking the same thing."

Hope exploded in his chest. "You were? Because so was I. I wanted to ask you then, for more time, for a chance, but I didn't know where to start."

"Yes, well, it was the same for me." She didn't look happy. Shouldn't she look happy, now they'd both confessed that they wanted the same thing?

He didn't get it. "Well, then?" he prodded. "Sabra, what is the problem? You want more, you just said so. You want more and so do I." He dared a step closer.

She jerked back, whipping up a hand. "You don't understand. That was last year. Everything's different now."

"Why? I don't get it. We're still the same people."

"No. No, we're not." She shook her head wildly. "Everything's changed for me, since my dad died."

"Sabra…"

"No. Wait. Listen, please. I see things so differently. I understand now that I've been kidding myself, thinking someday I would find love and happiness with someone, with *you*."

"But you have it. You have me. I love you."

"Oh, please," she scoffed. "Love and happiness? They just end, Matthias. They end and they leave you alone, with nothing. They leave you a shell of who you were, leave you just getting through the endless days, waiting for the time when it doesn't hurt anymore. And I, well, I can't. I just can't."

"But you said—"

"This." She talked right over him, lifting

both hands out to her sides in an encompassing gesture, one that seemed to include him and the cabin, the clearing, the forest, the whole of the small world they shared over Christmas. "*This* is all I have in me. This is all it will ever be. I can never give you anything more and if you need something more, well, then you need to go out and get it."

Sabra glared at Matthias. And he just stared at her—a hurt look, and angry, too.

Well, fine. Let him stare. Let him be angry, as angry as she was—that he'd done this, that he'd sprung this on her. She couldn't take this. She didn't know how to deal.

At the same time, deep within her, a small voice chided that she was way overreacting, that her emotions were knocked all out of whack by her grief over her dad.

She felt so much for the man standing in

front of her, felt desire and affection, felt *love*. Yeah. She did. She felt love, deep and strong. She didn't want to lose him.

But she *was* losing him. She *would* lose him. That was how life was—shining moments of joy and beauty, followed by a loneliness that killed.

Considering a future with him right now? It was like trying to decide what to do about the farm. She couldn't go back there and she couldn't let go of it. It was all mixed up together—the farm, Matthias, her dad.

Her dad, who was gone now. She missed him so much and she despised herself for that, for daring to miss him, when she hadn't been there for him during the last, lonely years of his life.

She'd left him to waste away on his own when he needed her most.

And this, with Matthias, well, what more was there to say? "I really do have to go."

Matt got the message. He got it loud and clear.

She'd cut him off at the knees, wrecked him but good. She had to go?

Terrific. He wanted her out of there, wanted *not* to be looking into those big, wounded eyes.

He reached out and pulled open the door to the Subaru. "Drive safe, Sabra." The words tasted like sawdust in his mouth. Still, he did wish her well. "You take care of yourself."

She stared at him, her eyes bigger than ever, her face much too pale. And then, slowly, she nodded. "You, too." She got in behind the wheel.

This is how it ends, he thought. No goodbye kiss, no hope that there ever might be more.

Not so much as a mention of next year.

There probably wouldn't be a next year—not for the two of them, together. Somehow, he was going to have to learn to accept that.

After this, well, what was there to come back for? He wanted more and she didn't. Really, where did they go from here?

He shut the door, called to his dog and went up the steps to the cabin without once looking back.

Chapter Ten

Sabra, the following March...

She didn't know what had come over her, re-ally.

A...lightening. A strange sense of promise where for months there had been nothing but despair.

On the spur of the moment, she took four days off work in the middle of the month and drove up to the farm. Nils and Marjorie were at their house when she pulled into the yard.

They ran out to greet her, grabbing her in tight hugs, saying what a nice surprise it was to see her. Meaning it, too.

Marjorie took her out to see the lambs. She also met with Nils for a couple of hours. They went over the books, discussed the upcoming market season. Soon, they would be planting blueberries, raspberries, blackberries and strawberries. They talked about the huge number of turkey orders for Thanksgiving—so many, in fact, that they'd already had to stop taking them. Next year, Nils planned to raise more birds.

Sabra joined Marjorie and Nils for dinner. Later, alone in the main house, she wandered the rooms. A cleaning team came in every three weeks to keep things tidy, so the place was in okay shape. But the greenhouse window in the kitchen needed someone to put a few potted plants in there and then take care of them.

And really, when you came right down to it, a kitchen remodel wouldn't hurt, either. In time. And a paint job, definitely. The old homestead could do with a general freshening-up if she ever intended to live here again.

Live here again?

Where had that idea come from?

She shook her head and put the thought from her mind.

That night, she slept in her old room, a dreamless, peaceful sort of sleep—or mostly dreamless, anyway.

Just before dawn she woke and realized she'd been dreaming of Matthias, a simple dream. They were here, in the farmhouse, together. In her dream, they went out to the front porch and sat in the twin rockers her dad had found years ago at a yard sale and refinished himself. Zoya snoozed at their feet.

Sabra sat up in bed, stretched, yawned and

looked out the window where the pink fingers of morning light inched across the horizon. Shoving back the covers, she ran over there, pushed the window up and breathed in the cool morning smell of new grass and damp earth.

Spring was here. Already. And leaning on the sill she felt…close. To her mother and her father, to all the generations of Bonds before her.

The idea dawned like the new morning.

She didn't want to sell the farm.

She wanted to move home to stay.

Sabra, that July…

"So just track him down," insisted Iris. "You blew it and you need to reach out, tell him you messed up, that your head was all turned around over your dad dying. You need to beg him for another chance."

"I can't." Sabra dropped a stack of folded clothes into an open box.

"Can't?" Iris scoffed. "Won't. That's what you really mean."

"It wouldn't be right to him," said Sabra.

"Oh, yeah, it would. It's the rightest thing in the world, telling a man who loves you that you love him, too, and want to be with him."

They were at Sabra's apartment—Sabra, Iris and Peyton, too. Sabra was moving home to the farm and her friends were pitching in, helping her pack up to go.

She tried to make Iris understand. "It wasn't our deal to go looking for each other, to go butting into each other's regular lives. If I want to change the agreement, I need to do it when I see him, at Christmas."

"Who says you'll see him at Christmas?"

"Well, what I mean is that next Christmas

would be the time to try again, if that's even possible anymore."

Iris shook her head. "Uh-uh. Not buying. You're just making excuses not to step up right now and get straight with the man you love."

Peyton emerged from the closet, her arms full of clothes. "Honey, I'm with Iris on this one." She dropped the clothes on the bed for Sabra to box up. "You screwed up. You need to fix it."

"And I will. At Christmas. I still have the key. I'll show up, as always, and I'll pray that he does, too."

Iris put both hands to her head and made an exploding gesture. "Wrong. Bad. You need to act now. He could find someone else in the next five months."

"He could have found someone else already," Sabra said, something inside of her dying a little at the very thought. "I *told* him to find someone else. I can't go breaking our rules and chasing after him now. If he's found someone new, I've got no right to try to get in the middle of that. I've got no right and I *won't*."

Iris opened her mouth to argue some more, but Peyton caught her eye and shook her head. "It's your call," Iris conceded at last. "But just for the record, I think you're making a big mistake."

Matt, early August...

Friday night at Beach Street Brews was as crowded and loud as ever. Matt was glad to be out, though. Sometimes a guy needed a beer, a bar full of people, and some mediocre rock and roll played at earsplitting levels.

The noise and party atmosphere distracted him, kept him from brooding over Sabra. It had been seven months since she'd made it painfully clear that they were going nowhere. Not ever. He needed to get over her, to get over *himself.*

It was past time for him to stop being an emo idiot and move the hell on. Life was too damn short to spend it longing for a woman who would never give him more than a holiday hookup. He was ready, after all these years, for a real relationship.

And damn it, he was through letting the important things pass him by.

Jerry, across the table from him, leaned in. "Someone's been asking to meet you." Jerry tipped his red head at two pretty women, a blonde and a brunette, as they approached their booth. "The blonde," said Jerry. "Mary's her name…"

The two women reached the booth. Jerry scooted over and patted the empty space next to him. The brunette sat down.

The blonde smiled shyly at Matt. "Matt Bravo," he said.

Her smile got brighter. "Mary Westbrook."

He moved over toward the wall and Mary slid in beside him.

They started talking, Matt and Mary. She'd gone to Valentine Bay High, graduated the same year as his sister Aislinn. Now Mary worked as a physical therapist at a local clinic. She had sky-blue eyes, a great laugh and an easy, friendly way about her.

No, she wasn't Sabra.

But Matt liked her. He liked her a lot.

Early November...

Matt sat on the sofa in his brother Daniel's study at the Bravo family house on Rhinehart Hill. Across the room, beyond his brother's big desk, the window that looked out over the front porch framed a portrait in fall colors, the maples deep red, the oaks gone to gold. Daniel's fourteen-month-old twins, Jake and Frannie, were upstairs with their latest nanny. Sometimes it was hard to believe how big those kids were now, and that it had been over a year since they lost Lillie.

A glass of scotch in each hand, Daniel came and sat in the armchair across the low table from Matt. He handed Matt a glass and offered a toast. "To you, Matt. And to the new woman in your life."

"Thanks." Matt touched his glass to his brother's and sipped. The scotch was excellent, smoky and hot going down.

Daniel took a slow sip, too. "I've been instructed to inform you that we all expect to be meeting Mary at Thanksgiving."

Matt chuckled. "Instructed, huh?"

Daniel didn't crack a smile. But then, he

rarely did. "We have four sisters, in case you've forgotten."

"Sisters," Matt kidded back. "Right. I vaguely remember them, yeah."

"They're all pleased to learn you've met someone special. They want to get to know her. Connor and Liam do, too." Connor and Liam were third- and fourth-born in the family, respectively. "And so do I."

"Well, Aislinn has already been after me to bring Mary." The truth was, he'd hesitated over inviting Mary. "I was kind of thinking it was too soon, you know?"

Daniel said, "It's never too soon if you really like someone."

An image took shape in his mind. It wasn't of Mary and he ordered it gone. "Well, good. I did invite her. She said yes. Mary's looking forward to meeting the family."

"I'm glad. And I'm happy for you..."

Two days later...

Unbuttoning his uniform shirt as he went, Matt led the way into his bedroom, Zoya hopping along behind. She stretched out on the rug by the bed and panted up at him contentedly as he finished getting out of his work clothes and stuffed them in the hamper.

That night, he was taking Mary out to eat and then to a stand-up comedy show at the Valentine Bay Theatre. He grabbed a pair of jeans from a drawer, tossed them across the bed and went to the closet for a shirt to wear under his jacket.

When he grabbed the blue button-down off the rod, he caught sight of a corner of this year's Wild and Scenic Oregon calendar still tacked to the wall. The hangers clattered loudly along the rod as he shoved them back, hard.

Why had he even bought the damn thing

this year—and not only bought it, but for several months, continued crossing off the days?

Apparently, for some men, being told to forget it was just never enough.

The calendar was turned to October, with a view of the Deschutes National Forest in fall. Below the beautiful picture of trees in autumn, the calendar page itself showed not a single red X. He'd stopped marking the days the month before.

And why was he keeping it? The calendar was of zero use or interest to him now.

He yanked it off the wall. The tack went flying. He heard it bounce on the closet floor, somewhere he'd probably step on it in bare feet one day soon.

Too bad. He didn't have time to crawl around looking for it now. Carrying the shirt in one hand and the calendar in the other, he ducked out of the closet. Marching straight to the dresser, he tossed the calendar in the wastebasket there. Then he dropped the shirt on the bed with his jeans and turned for the bathroom to grab a quick shower.

Sabra, early December...

In downtown Astoria, the shop windows and the streets were all decked out for Christmas. Acres of lighted garland bedecked with shiny ornaments and bells looped between the streetlights. Live trees in pots lined the sidewalk, each one lit up and hung with bright decorations.

At the corner, a lone musician played "White Christmas" on a xylophone. Sabra paused with a few other bundled-up shoppers to listen to the tune. When the song came to an end, she tossed a dollar in the open case at the musician's feet. Pulling her heavy jacket a little closer against the winter chill, she crossed the street and continued on to midway along the next block.

The store she sought was called Sugar and Spice. Like every other shop on the street, it had Christmas displays in the front windows, scenes of festively dressed mannequins, ones that were definitely more spicy than sweet. One mannequin wore a sexy elf costume and another, a red thong sewn with tiny, winking party lights. One had her hands bound behind her back with handcuffs, a Santa hat slipping sexily over one eye while a male mannequin in a leather jockstrap and policeman's hat tickled her with a giant green feather.

Inside, the girl behind the counter wore a skimpy Mrs. Santa Claus costume and a gray wig topped by a crown of Christmas tree lights. "Hey. What can I help you with?"

"Just looking…" Sabra headed for the racks of revealing lingerie.

Sexy Mrs. Claus followed her over there. "Are you wanting anything in particular?"

Help from an expert?

Really, what could it hurt? "It's like this," Sabra said as she checked through the bra-and-panty sets. "I'm in—or at least, I've *been* in—this wonderful relationship. But we aren't together all the time. We meet up for several days, once a year."

Mrs. Claus looked confused. "What's the kink?"

Sabra laughed. "It's just once a year, over Christmas, no contact otherwise. Is that a kink?"

Mrs. Claus let that question go. "Let me try again. So…there's a problem in this relation-ship?"

"Well, the thing is, last year it ended badly and it was all my fault."

Mrs. Claus made a soft, sympathetic sound. "Oh, no."

"Yeah. And, see, I don't want to break our rules. I'm not going to stalk the guy. But this year, I'll be there at the usual place and time in case he does show. I'm going to knock myself out to make things right, make it..."

"More?" suggested Mrs. Claus.

Sabra paused in her impatient flicking from one panty set to the next. "More. Yes. That's it. I want more with him. Last year, he was already there in the *more* department. He wanted to take the biggest chance of all with me. But I wasn't ready. I said some things that I wish I hadn't. It's very likely he took what I said to mean it was over between us. And now, I only want a prayer that he might be willing to give me another shot. I don't need handcuffs or a latex suit. I just want to feel confident. If he shows up and I get lucky enough to make it as far as taking off my clothes…"

"You want him wowed." Mrs. Claus had that look, the one a sales professional gets when she finally understands exactly what her customer is shopping for. "You don't want to role-play or try something new. You just want to be you, the sexiest possible you."

Sabra grabbed an itty-bitty black satin number, held it up and joked, "You don't happen to have this in camo?"

Mrs. Claus's smile was slow and also triumphant. "As a matter of fact, we do."

Sabra bought the sexy camo undies and several other seductive bits of lace and satin. She knew that cute underwear wasn't the answer to anything, really. If Matthias was through with her, a see-through bra wouldn't change his mind.

And yet, she felt hopeful and excited.

She was ready to go all in with him, at last. All he had to do was show up this year and she would pull out all the stops to get just one more chance with him.

December 23, last year...

Sabra's heart just about detonated in her chest when she turned the last corner and rolled into the clearing. Matthias, in a uniform that looked identical to the one his friend Jerry had been wearing when he stopped by the year before, leaned back against the tailgate of a state trooper patrol truck.

He's here! He came!

For a few glorious, too-brief seconds, she knew she was getting the second chance she'd longed for, that this year, she was going to make everything come out right.

She pulled her car to a stop several feet back from the man and the truck.

About then, in the silence that followed turning off the engine, she started putting it together.

This was all wrong.

No lights in the cabin, Matthias in his uniform, with a mud-splattered state police vehicle behind him. No Zoya. No gorgeous Christmas tree tied to a rack on the roof.

And he hadn't moved yet. He remained at the tailgate, big arms across his chest, his hat shading his eyes.

Her hands shook and her stomach pitched and rolled. She sat there in the driver's seat, her heart hurling itself madly against the wall of her chest, unable to move for a good count of ten.

But this was her show, now wasn't it? She could already see that he wasn't planning a tender reunion. If she didn't want to talk to him, she ought to start the engine again and drive away.

That seemed the less painful option in the short run—and also the one that would always leave her wondering, leave her hanging. Leave her wishing she'd asked him straight out for another chance.

If he said no, well, *Goodbye* was an actual word. And she needed to hear him say it out loud.

First step: get out of the damn car.

But still she didn't move. Her mind sparked wildly, impulses firing madly, going off like bottle rockets in her brain, shooting along the endless network of nerves in her body, leading her exactly nowhere.

Grabbing the latch with shaking fingers, she gave it a yank.

The door opened and she swung her legs

out, rising without pausing to steady herself. Surprisingly, she didn't go pitching over face-down in the dirt.

She was on her feet and moving toward him. A couple of yards away from him, she stopped. He swiped off his hat. The pain in her chest was damn near unbearable.

His blue eyes told her nothing. They *gave* her nothing.

The sun was out, of all things. It brought out the silvery threads in his dark blond hair. He was so beautiful, all square-jawed and un-compromising, with that broad chest and those big arms she wanted wrapped good and hard around her.

Not mine. The two words ripped through her brain like a buzz saw. Whatever they'd had, it was gone now. He was not hers and he never would be.

She'd had her chance and she hadn't been

ready. It was no one's fault, really. Timing did matter and hers had been seriously bad. "I take it you're not staying."

Matt had dreaded this moment.

He'd known that whatever happened—if she showed, if she didn't—it was going to be bad.

But this—the very sight of her, the stricken look on her face—it was worse than he'd ever imagined it could be.

"I didn't really expect you to show," he said. The words felt cruel as they fell from his lips. He'd driven out here feeling angry and wronged, self-righteous. Ready to lay it on her that he'd taken her advice and found someone new, willing her to be here so he could have the final say.

But now, having simply watched her get out of her car and walk over to him, having looked her square in her beautiful face, all that sanctimonious fury had drained out of him. He had no anger left to sustain him.

"I'm on duty," he said.

"Uh, yeah. I kind of figured that."

"But I came by just in case you showed up, so you wouldn't wonder—I mean, you know. Be left hanging."

"Thank you." The skin was too pale around her soft lips. He needed to reach for her, hold her, soothe her.

He wrapped both arms across his chest good and tight, the hat dangling from between the fingers of his right hand. It was the only way to keep himself from grabbing her close.

Spit it out, you SOB. Just say it. "I've met someone."

"Ah." The sound was so soft. Full of pain. And understanding. Two bright spots of color flamed high on her cheeks. He was hurting her, hurting her so bad.

What she'd done to him last year? It was nothing compared to what he was putting her through now.

He needed to explain himself, he realized, needed to say something *real* to her, something true, from his heart. "Sabra, I swear to you, I never would have moved on."

She swallowed convulsively and gave him a sharp nod. "Yeah." It came out a ragged little whisper. "I know that. I do."

"You were so insistent. So sure."

"Yes. You're right. I was."

"You *told* me to find someone else."

"And you did." She smiled. It seemed to take a lot of effort. "I'm, um, glad for you. I want you to be happy, Matthias, I honestly do."

"You have meant so much to me," he said, striving for the right words, the true words, from his heart. "More than I seem to know how to say."

* * *

Kind, Sabra thought. *He's trying so hard to be kind.*

So why did it feel like he was ripping her heart out?

Worst of all, she got it. She saw it so clearly. What he was doing to her now was essentially what she'd done to him a year ago.

She'd hurt him, told him outright he would never have what he longed for from her. He'd done what he had to do to get over her. She knew she had no one to blame but herself.

Now she just needed to hold it together, get through this with some small shred of dignity intact.

She was about to open her mouth and wish him well with his new love—and the words got clogged in her throat.

Because she just couldn't.

If another woman loved him now and did it

well and fully, well, all right then. He should be with that woman.

But to completely give up, right here and now?

She just wasn't that good of a person. "I have a request."

"Name it."

"I have the key and I'll give it to you if that's how you want it. But I'm asking you to let me keep it for one more year. Let me keep it and I will be here, same time as always, next year. If you're still with your new love, just stay away till the sun is down. If you don't show by dark, that will be all I need to know. I'll lock up and push the key under the door. You'll never see me again."

There was more. So much more she needed to say, including the most important words…

I love you, Matthias. I love you and I should have said so last year.

But she hadn't. Instead, she'd told him to find someone else. And now they were here, in the cold December sunlight, saying goodbye. And she had no right at all to speak her love out loud.

She shut her mouth and waited, certain he would say that he wanted his key back and he wanted it right now.

But he only stood there, holding his hat, arms folded hard against her, his expression blank, those beautiful eyes of his so guarded.

Time stretched out on a razor's edge of loss and misery. She tried to reassure herself.

He wasn't asking for the key back, was he? That was a good sign.

Wasn't it?

She almost let herself feel the faintest glimmer of hope.

But then he broke the awful silence. "Goodbye, Sabra."

And with that, he put his hat back on and turned on his heel, heading for the driver's side of the pickup. She just stood there, afraid to move for fear she would shatter.

He got in, turned the engine on, circled the cabin and disappeared down the twisting dirt road.

She held it together, barely, until the sound of his engine faded away in the distance.

Then her knees stopped working. With a strangled cry, she sank to a crouch. "Get up," she muttered, disgusted with herself.

But it was no good. Her heart was aching so bad and there was really no alternative but to give herself up to the pain.

At least he was gone. He wouldn't have to see this.

It was just her and her broken heart, the bitter taste of regret on her tongue.

Wrapping her arms around herself, Sabra

gave in completely. Slowly, she toppled onto her side. Curling up into herself on the cold winter ground, she let her tears fall.

Chapter Eleven

Sabra, the following March…

"This kitchen is gorgeous," Peyton declared from her favorite spot at Sabra's new chef-quality stove. "You did it all. The farm sink, these quartz counters. Clean white cabinets with all the storage options and inner drawers. I'm so jealous."

Sabra, sitting at the island next to Iris, sipped her wine. "You saw it before. A bad memory from the early '80s. Uh-uh. It was crying out for an update and we've been doing better than ever since I finally moved home and started tackling my job here, day-to-day. I've hooked us up with two new restaurants, big accounts. It all helps—and you, my dear Peyton, are invited to make your magic in my new kitchen anytime." The wonderful smell of Peyton's special pasta sauce graced the air. "You, too." Sabra elbowed Iris playfully and then raised her wineglass. "Just bring more of this wine with you when you come."

An hour later, they sat on the long benches at the harvest table her great-grandfather had built and shared the meal Peyton had cooked for them. It wasn't until they'd taken their coffee into the living room that Sabra's friends started in on her about the "cabin guy" and how she needed to get over him.

Iris insisted, "You can't spend the whole year just sitting around waiting on a guy who's with someone else and only showed up last year to say goodbye."

Pain, fresh and sharp, stabbed through her at the thought of that too-bright December day. "Who says I'm just sitting around? I've got a farm to run."

"Please, girlfriend. We're not talking about work and you know we're not. We're talking about your social life, which is essentially nonexistent."

"Wait a minute. I have *you* guys. I have other friends, too, longtime friends I grew up with. We've reconnected since I moved home and we get together now and then, meet up for a show or lunch, or whatever."

"You do hear yourself," Peyton chimed in. "*Friends*, you said."

"We are talking *men*," said Iris. "And not men *friends*. Uh-uh. You owe yourself at least a few hot nights, some seriously sexy times."

"That's not going to happen. It's not who I am and I'm fine with that."

"Just download a few dating apps," Peyton pleaded.

"FarmersOnly.com, for crying out loud," moaned Iris.

"But I—"

"No." Iris shook a finger at her. "No excuses. Even if everything goes the way you hope it will next Christmas, even if it's over with the other woman, if he drops to his knees and begs for one more chance with you—that changes nothing. You *owe* that man nothing. From now until then is a long time. You owe it to *yourself* to make good use of that time."

"Make *use* of it?" Sabra scoffed. "What does that even mean?"

"It means that you went from Stan the Swine to James the Jerk to once a year with the cabin guy. It's not going to kill you to step out of your comfort zone and see what's out there. You need to mix it up a little. You just might find a man who's as ready for you as you are for him."

"But I *told* you. Matthias *was* ready. *I* messed it up."

"Don't you dare blame yourself." Iris was nothing if not loyal. "You'd lost your *dad*. That man you're pining for now could have been a *little* more understanding."

"And you've already boxed yourself in," Peyton chided. "You won't contact the guy before Christmas."

"I told you, that's our agreement and—"

"Understood." Peyton cut her off, but in a gentle tone. "My point is, there's nothing more you can do for now in terms of Matthias."

"So?"

"So, it's a lot of months until December. Make those months count, that's all we're saying."

"It's a numbers game," declared Iris. "You've got to get out there and kiss a lot of toads before you're ever going to meet the right guy for you."

"I've already met the right guy," Sabra said quietly, knowing in her deepest heart that it was true. "I've met the right guy—and he's with someone else now."

Her friends shook their heads.

They sipped their coffee in silence for a few seconds.

"Just try," Peyton urged softly at last. "A few dates, that's all. Give some other guy a shot."

Sabra wasn't exactly sure how they'd done it. But Peyton and Iris had prevailed. She had three dating apps on her phone now.

And she made an effort. She truly did. She filled out her profile information in detail, honestly. And she asked Marjorie, who had a certain aptitude with a digital camera, to take some good pictures of her which she posted with her profiles.

And then she started interacting, reaching out to guys whose profiles and pictures looked interesting, responding when someone reached out to her. She went with her instincts. If a guy seemed creepy or catfishy, she let him know she wasn't interested and moved on.

Truth to tell, none of them *really* interested her. Because she wanted Matthias and she just plain *wasn't* interested.

When she'd failed to so much as meet a guy for coffee by the end of April, Iris gave her a pep talk about not trying hard enough, about the need to get out there, in real life.

Sabra knew her friend had a point. There was trying—and there was *really* trying. Yeah, she'd put up the profiles and interacted a little online, but nothing more.

And that made her kind of an internet dating jerk, now didn't it? She wasn't benching or breadcrumbing anyone. She was simply wasting the time of the men she right-swiped. She needed to do better, make a real effort, if only to prove to herself that there wasn't some unknown guy waiting out there who was just right for her, a guy who could have her asking, *Matthias Bravo, who?*

Could that ever actually happen?

No. Uh-uh. She knew with absolute certainty that it couldn't.

However, more than once in her life she'd been totally wrong. Romantically speaking, at this point in time, she was 0 for 3. What did she know, really, about any of this?

Sabra kept at it.

No, she wasn't ready to get up close and in person with these guys she was making contact with online. But at least by mid-May, she'd stepped up her game from mere messaging to Skype and FaceTime. It was so much easier to eliminate a guy once she'd seen him in action, heard his voice while his mouth was moving—and there she went again, thinking in terms of eliminating a man rather than trying really hard to meet someone new.

Finally, in June, she did it, took a giant step forward.

She agreed to meet a nice guy named Dave at the Astoria Farmer's Market. Dave seemed every bit as nice in person as he had during their messaging phase and on FaceTime. Too bad there was zero spark. None. A complete and utter lack of chemistry.

Worse, she felt like she was cheating on Matthias.

As they reached the last booth, Dave asked her out to dinner that night.

She turned him down. Dave got the message. She never heard from him again. Which was all for the best.

She did coffee dates after that. Several of them. During each one, she nursed a latte and wished she was anywhere but there.

She went out with a podiatrist who talked really fast and all about himself through a very expensive dinner. Then later, on the sidewalk outside the restaurant, he grabbed her and tried to choke her with his tongue down her throat. Somehow, she resisted the urge to smack his self-absorbed face and simply told him never to try anything like that again with her.

He called her a tease and a few other uglier names. And then, of all things, he grabbed her hand, kissed it and apologized profusely.

She said, "Apology accepted. Just please, never contact me again."

After the podiatrist, she took a break from

dating. She figured she needed it. Deserved it, even.

Then, in late September, on Compatible-Mate.com, she met a lawyer named Ted.

They went out to a concert and she had a good time. When he kissed her at her door, it was…pleasant.

And pleasant was pretty awful. A man's kiss should be much more than *pleasant*, or what was the point?

Still, that's what Ted's kiss was. Pleasant.

She experienced none of the goodness the right kiss always brings—no shivers racing up and down her spine, no galloping heart, no fireworks whatsoever. In fact, what she felt was a deep sadness, a longing for Matthias.

But Ted really did seem like a great guy. She liked him.

He asked her out again two weeks later and she said yes to dinner and a show. That time, when he kissed her as they were saying good-night, she knew beyond any doubt that she never wanted to kiss him again.

And when he called her a few nights later to ask her out for Friday night, she knew she should turn him down, tell him how much she liked him, explain somehow that merely liking him wasn't enough, that she was wasting his time and that wasn't right.

But there was nothing *wrong* with him—other than the simple fact that he wasn't Matthias. In no way was that Ted's fault.

She opened her mouth to express her regrets—and a yes fell out.

They went to dinner again. Ted seemed happy. Buoyant, even. He talked about his firm and how well he was doing there. He asked about the farm and he actually seemed interested when she proudly described the orchard of sapling fruit trees they'd put in that spring.

Over dessert, Ted leaned across the table, his dark eyes gleaming, a happy grin on his handsome face. "I have to tell you. I never thought this would work for me. But Sabra, now I've found you, I'm changing my mind about meeting someone online. I know we haven't really taken it to the next level, so to speak. But still. This is special, what's happening between us. Don't you feel it? Here we are on date three and I'm honestly thinking we're going somewhere."

Going somewhere?

No way.

Sabra kind of hated herself at that moment. She knew she had to stop this, that she had no right to go one second longer without getting real with the guy. "I'm sorry, Ted."

He sat back. "Sorry?"

"The truth is, you and I are never reaching the next level. We're going nowhere. I'm in love with someone else and I can't do this anymore."

Ted's eyes were no longer gleaming. "Tell me something, Sabra," he said, cool and flat. "If you're in love with someone else, why the hell aren't you with him—and you know what?" He shoved back his chair and plunked his napkin on the table. "Don't answer that because I don't even care."

Muttering invectives against online dating in general and, more specifically, crazy women who mess with a guy's mind, he headed for the door.

With a sigh, Sabra signaled for the check.

Late October...

"I'm done, you guys," Sabra said. "Finished. Not going there—online or otherwise. Because you know what? Ted was right. It's wrong to use one guy to try to forget another. And I'm never doing that again."

Her friends regarded her solemnly from the other side of her harvest table. "We do get it," admitted Peyton.

Iris, as always, asked the hardest question. "What will you do if he doesn't show in December?"

Her heart broke all over again at the very thought. But she drew herself up straight. "Die a little. Suffer a lot—and please don't look so worried. I love Matthias. I want him. No one else but him. I have to go all the way with that first. If he's not there on December twenty-third, *that's* when I'll have to figure out what comes next." She looked from one dear face to the other. "I know. I get it. I mean, who does what he and I have done? What two sane people make an agreement to have each other just for the holidays—and then keep that agreement for years? I know that sounds batcrap crazy, I do. But it worked for us. It was what we both needed. Our agreement created the space we both required, the time and patience to learn to love again. I truly believe that if my dad hadn't died, Matthias and I would be married by now. But he did die and that threw everything into chaos for me. Matthias asked me for more and I answered no, unequivocally. I told him never. I said if he wanted more, he needed to go and find someone else. Which brought us here."

"Matthias should have waited," grumbled Iris, swiping a tear from her cheek. "He should have given you more space."

"Space? I had *years* of space. And he did wait. I knew it. I felt it, the year before I lost my dad. I knew he wanted more that year and *I* wanted more, too. But neither of us stepped up and said so. Still, when we parted that year, I knew that the next year, we would be taking it further. That didn't happen because the next year, I was a mess. But he *had* waited. He'd waited out that whole year."

Peyton said sheepishly, "Honey, we just want you to be prepared, you know? Just in case he, well, I mean…" Her voice trailed off.

Sabra put it right out there. "You honestly don't think he's going to be there, do you?" Both of her friends remained silent. But the truth was in their eyes. Peyton glanced away. And Iris gave a sad little shrug. Sabra said firmly, "There is no preparing for that. If he doesn't show, for me it's going to be as bad as it was last Christmas."

"But…" Peyton swallowed hard. "I mean, you *will* get through it, right? You'll be okay?"

Sabra did understand the deeper implications of the question. And she loved her friends all the more for venturing into this difficult territory. "I adored my dad. I miss him every day and I wish I'd done more to help him live without my mom. In many ways, I'm like him. A total romantic, devoted until death. But I'm like my mom, too. And my mom was stronger than my dad was, strong *and* practical." Sabra reached across the rough wood surface of the old table.

Her friends were there to meet her. Peyton's hand settled on hers and then Iris's hand covered Peyton's.

"You'll make it through, one way or another," said Iris. "That's what you're telling us, right?"

"One way or another, yes. If he doesn't show, I may curl up in a fetal position and cry my eyes out just like I did last year. I may spend a lot of time being depressed and self-indulgent. I may be miserable for months. It's possible that, after being with him, knowing him, *loving* him, there's just no one else for me, that he's it for me, the one. Whatever happens, though, however it ends up with him this year, I promise you both that I will make it through."

December 23, this year...

An emotional wreck.

That described Sabra's condition exactly as she drove toward the cabin. An emotional wreck who almost ended up an *actual* wreck. Twice.

She kept spacing off, praying he would be there, then *certain* he would be there. And then *knowing* absolutely that she was deluding herself completely. He wasn't going to be there and how would she bear it?

It was during one of those spaced-out moments that a deer bolted out into the road and then stopped stock-still and stared at her through her windshield, as if to say, *Whoa. A car. Where'd that come from?*

She slammed on the brakes and skidded to a stop just in time. The deer—a nice buck, a six pointer—stared at her for a good ten seconds more before leaping off into the brush again.

She took her foot off the brake and carefully steered to the shoulder of the road, where she dropped her forehead to the steering wheel and waited for her heart to stop trying to punch its way out of her chest.

When her mouth no longer tasted like old pennies and her hands had stopped shaking, she set out again.

The second almost-wreck happened after she'd turned off the highway into the woods, onto the series of unimproved roads that would finally take her to the cabin and her own personal moment of truth. Really, she didn't know what happened that second time. She was looking at the road, both hands on the wheel.

But her mind? Her heart? Her whole being?

Elsewhere, far away, lost in memories of Christmases past. Of nights on the porch in a world buried in snow, of his hands—so big and yet deft and quick, whittling a small piece of wood into a porcupine, just for her, touching her naked body, showing her all the ways he could make her moan.

The giant tree seemed to rise up in front of her out of nowhere. With a shriek, she slammed the brakes again, sliding on the dirt road, her heartbeat so loud in her ears it sounded like drums, her whole body gone strangely tingly and numb with the sheer unreality of what was happening.

By some miracle, she eased the wheel to the right with the slide of gravel beneath her tires.

The Subaru cleared the tree by mere inches. She came to a stop with the tree looming in her side window.

After that near-death experience, she turned off the engine, slumped back in her seat, shut her eyes and reminded herself that she'd promised Iris and Peyton she would get through this, one way or another. It would be so wrong for her to end up a statistic—especially if she finished herself off before even getting to the cabin and finding out that, just maybe, the man she hoped to meet there had shown up ready to try again, exactly as she dreamed he might.

He could be there right this minute, waiting to take her in his arms and swear that from this day forward, she was his only one.

Oh, if only that could really happen.

She was on fire to be the one for him, to claim him as hers. She yearned for this to be it, *their* year, the year they finally built something more than a beautiful Christmas together.

But none of that was even possible if she didn't keep her eyes on the road and get her ass to the cabin.

She started up the car again and put it in gear.

Five minutes later, her spirits hit a new low. The suspense was unbearable. And she really should face reality.

Her friends were right. Matthias had found someone else and she needed to accept that. She needed to stop this idiocy and find a way to move on as she'd once told him to do.

She should give up this foolishness, she kept thinking, give it up and go home. There was no point. She was only driving toward more heartbreak.

But she didn't turn around.

When she reached the last stretch of dirt road leading up to the cabin, her heart was hammering so hard and so fast, she worried it might just explode from her body. They would find her days from now, the front end of the Outback crunched against a tree, her lifeless form slumped in the seat, a gaping, empty hole in the middle of her chest.

She rounded the last curve and the cabin came into view.

Her nearly-exploded heart stopped dead—and then began beating again faster than ever as she pulled to a stop behind the muddy Jeep.

The gray world had come alive again. With anticipation. With promise. With her love that filled her up and overflowed, bringing the woods and the clearing, the rustic cabin, even the car in which she sat, into sharper focus, everything so vivid, in living color.

She heard a gleeful laugh. It was her own. "Yes!" she cried aloud. "Yes, yes, yes!"

Oh, it was perfect. The best moment ever. Her seemingly hopeless dream, finally, at last, coming true.

Golden light shone from the windows and smoke curled lazily from the stone chimney, drifting upward toward the gray sky. She managed to turn off the engine.

And then she just sat there, barely breathing, unable to move, still marginally terrified that she was reading this all wrong, that the man inside the cabin wasn't really waiting there for her.

Until the front door swung open.

And at last, after so long—*too* long, forever and a day—she saw him.

So tall and broad, in camo pants, boots and a mud-colored shirt, his dirty-blond hair a little longer than last year, every inch of him powerful, strong, muscular. Cut.

Joy burst like a blinding light inside her as her gaze met his. She saw it all then. In the blue fire of his eyes, in his slow, welcoming smile.

Mine, she thought. *All mine. As I am his. At last.*

Chapter Twelve

He came for her, moving fast down the porch steps, boots eating up the distance between them, eyes promising everything.

Love. Heat. Wonder. The kind of bond that weathers the worst storms. Joy and laughter and the two of them, together, forever and ever, building a family, making a rich and meaningful life.

She threw open her door just as he reached her. Popping the seat belt latch, she flung herself toward him.

He caught her, those strong arms going around her. She landed on her feet against his broad, hard chest.

"Oh, thank God…" They breathed the prayerful words in unison. And then his beautiful mouth crashed down on hers.

The clean, man-and-cedar scent of him was all around her, encompassing her, exciting her even more. The kiss grew deeper, and his hold on her got tighter.

One minute, she had her two feet on the ground and the next, he swept her up against his chest, still kissing her, still holding her the way she'd dreamed he might again someday.

Like she was his and he was hers and he would never, ever let her go. He turned for the house, kissing her as he went.

Up the steps he took her, through the open door.

The scent of evergreen intensified as he kicked the door shut. He'd already brought the tree in and propped it up in the stand. Zoya lay by the fire, panting a little. She rolled over inviting a belly scratch and let out a whine of greeting. Sabra saw the tree and the dog in fleeting glimpses, keeping her mouth locked to his, worshipping him with that kiss.

Matthias kept walking, carrying her across the rough boards of the floor, to the stairs and up them.

The kiss never broke.

Until he threw her on the bed. She bounced twice, laughing.

"Take everything off." His eyes made a million very sexy promises. "Do it fast."

Not a problem. Not in the least. They stripped in unison, clothes flying everywhere. She'd worn one of those sexy bra-and-panty sets she'd bought the year before, but she gave him no time to appreciate them. She tore them off and tossed them aside.

And he?

Oh, he was everything she remembered, all she longed for—honed and deep-chested, with those sculpted arms that took her breath away. Such a big man.

Everywhere.

She held up her arms to him and he came down to her, grabbing her close again, slamming his mouth on hers.

It was frantic and hungry, not smooth in the least. Needful and desperate, necessary as air. They rolled, their hands everywhere, relearning each other, every muscle, every secret curve. There were more kisses, deep ones that turned her heart inside out. His fingers found the core of her, so wet, so ready.

They needed more.

They needed everything, to be joined, each to the other.

He produced a condom seemingly from thin air.

"Planned ahead, did you?" she asked, trying to tease him, ending up sounding breathless and needy.

His eyes burned into hers. "I want this, Sabra. Us. I want it forever."

"Yes," she said, before he'd even finished asking. "Forever. You and me."

"Don't leave me. Don't do that again. Don't drive me away." He stroked her cheek.

"I won't. I swear it. I'm ready now, Matthias. Ready for the rest of our lives, you and me. I love you. You're the only one, and you always will be."

"Sabra…" He kissed her again, wildly, his fingers tunneling in her hair, his mouth demanding everything, all of her. "My love," he whispered against her parted lips. "I love you, always. I was such a fool."

"It's not as if you were the only fool." She broke away enough to plead, "Let me…" And she took the condom from him, removed the wrapper and carefully slid it on.

Once she had it in place, he lifted her as though she weighed nothing. Stretching out on his back, he set her down on top of him.

She was so ready. Beyond ready. Rising to her knees, she lined him up with her heat and took him inside—all the way, to the hilt.

He groaned and she bent to him, claiming his mouth with hers, rocking her hips on him in long, needful strokes. He clasped her bottom with those strong hands, one palm on each cheek, and moved with her, surging up into her, sending her reeling.

She came with a gleeful cry.

And then he was rolling them, taking the top position. Rising up over her, he pushed in deep and true.

That time, when her second finish shattered through her, he joined her. They cried out in unison, going over as one, holding each other, Matthias and Sabra.

Together.

At last.

An hour or two later, they went downstairs naked. She greeted Zoya and admired the tree.

He didn't let her linger in the main room long, though. Pulling her into the bathroom, he filled the tub, added bath salts, climbed in and crooked a finger at her to join him.

She did, eagerly, settling in between his legs, leaning back on him. He really did make the firmest, most supportive sort of pillow. For a while, they floated in the hot water that smelled of lemons and mint.

He told her that he had a missing sister.

"What? You're kidding me."

He nuzzled her hair. "Nope. This past year,

we found out that the oldest of my sisters, Aislinn, was switched at birth."

"So then, Aislinn isn't your sister by blood?"

"No. If she hadn't been switched, her name would be Madison Delaney."

"Wait." Sabra sat up, sending water sloshing. "Not *the* Madison Delaney, America's darling, the movie star?"

"Yes." Gently, Matthias pulled her back to rest against his chest. "We have a long-lost sister, and she is a movie star."

"Wow."

"Exactly. We've been trying to reach out to her. So far, our attempts have been rebuffed— either by her or by the people who protect her, we're not sure which."

"But you're not giving up." It wasn't a question.

He replied as she knew he would. "One way or another, we'll find a way to get through to her. As we will find Finn. Someday. Somehow..."

"I know you will," she whispered, and they were silent for a time.

But then, he bent his head to her and pressed his rough cheek to her smooth one. "Forever," he said gruffly. "I mean it. You still on for that?"

"Always." She lifted her arm from the water and reached back to slide her wet hand around the nape of his neck, tipping her head up to him for a quick kiss.

But one kiss from him? Never enough.

Already she could feel him, growing hard and ready, wanting her as she wanted him— again.

Sometime later, she told him that she'd moved back to the farm.

"When was that?" he asked.

"It's been a long time now. I moved in July, a year and a half ago."

He nuzzled her hair, which she'd piled on her head to keep it from getting too wet. "So then, you were already living there last Christmas, when I showed up just long enough to tell you it was over."

"Yeah."

He muttered something bleak. She couldn't make out the exact words, and she decided not to ask. Instead, she took his hand from the side of the tub and pulled it down into the water, across her stomach, so his arm was wrapped around her.

"Are you happy there, at your family's farm?" He bit the shell of her ear, so lightly, causing a thrilled little shiver to slide through her.

"Very." She slithered around, splashing water

everywhere, until she was face-to-face with him. "I'm hoping to stay there."

"Hoping?"

"Well, I want to be with you. And maybe you want to stay in Valentine Bay." He kissed the end of her nose and she backpedaled, "If I'm moving too fast for you—?"

"No way. There is no 'too fast' when it comes to you and me, not anymore. We've wasted too much time already." He took her slippery shoulders and pulled her up so he could claim her mouth in a lazy, thorough kiss. When he finally allowed her to sink back into the cooling water, he said, "Yes. I'll move to your farm with you."

She reached up, pressed her hand to his bristly cheek. "You haven't even seen the place yet."

"I don't need to see it. You've moved home and that makes you happy. I love you and for me, home is where you are. You've mentioned that your farm is in Astoria, which means my field office is nearby. Getting to work won't be an issue—and do you realize you've never told me the name of this farm of yours?"

"Berry Bog Farm."

"Perfect."

"What's perfect?"

"Everything." He traced her eyebrows, one and then the other. "I'm going to need your phone number as soon as we get out of this tub."

"You got it."

"I'm serious, Sabra. I won't let you leave this cabin, not even to sit on the porch, until your number is safe in my phone."

"I'll get right on that."

"You'd better," he warned, but when she started to climb from the tub, he held her there. "Not yet. In a little while."

With a sigh, she kissed his square chin. "This is kind of nice, you and me, naked in the tub together…"

"*Kind of nice* doesn't even come close." He pressed his wet hand to her cheek, then made a cradle of his index finger and lifted her chin so their eyes met. "The thing with Mary…?"

Her heart felt caged, suddenly, hurting in her too-small chest. "That's her name? Mary?"

He nodded. And then he pressed his forehead to hers and whispered, "I never should have started it with her. I was so hurt and mad at you."

She whispered her own confession. "I was so screwed up over my dad, screwed up and afraid, of you and me, of how powerful and good it was between us, of trusting what we have together—and then of someday losing you, like my dad lost my mom. So I told you to go out and look for what you needed. No way can I blame you for taking me at my word. I just hope… Oh, I don't know. I feel bad for her. For you. For all of it."

"It's been over with her for a year," he said. "A year, as of today."

She stared at him, confused. "You broke up with her on the twenty-third of *last* December?"

"That's right."

"The same day you drove up here to tell me you were with her?"

"That's the one."

"But I don't, I mean, how…?"

He pulled on a damp curl of her hair and then guided it tenderly behind her ear. "I knew it wouldn't work with her the minute I saw your face last year. I was just too damn stubborn to admit it right then. But as soon as I left you standing there alone, I knew what I had to do. I drove back to Valentine Bay feeling like a first-class jerk, wondering how I was going to break it to Mary that I couldn't be with her, that it was all wrong."

"Oh, Matt. And at the holidays, no less. What a mess I made. I'm so sorry."

But he gave her that wonderful, wry smile she loved so much. "It could have been worse. As it turned out, I didn't have to play the jerk, after all. Mary broke up with *me*."

She gasped. "No."

"Oh, yeah. We had a date to see a Christmas play that night. I went to pick her up and she asked me to come in for a minute. I stepped over the threshold—and then we just stood there by the door and she said how she'd been thinking, that it just wasn't working for her with me, that it wasn't love and she didn't feel it ever could be, that she and I needed to face the truth and move on. She really meant it," he said, his wry smile in evidence again. "We ended it right then, simple as that."

Sabra cradled his beard-scruffy cheek. "I do want to apologize sincerely, for hurting you, for sending you off to find someone else. I really messed that up. I could have lost you forever."

Matthias frowned. "I pushed too hard at the wrong time. You were all turned around over losing your dad. I wasn't patient and I should have been. As for losing me, you never could, not really. Somehow, I would always find my way back to you."

"And I. To you." They did that thing lovers do, having sex with their eyes. Then, with a happy sigh, she floated to her back once more and rested against him. "I have to ask…"

His warm breath stirred her hair as he pressed a kiss to the crown of her head. "Anything."

"All that time, from last Christmas to now. Did you know you would come to meet me today?"

"I did. No question, as sure as I knew I would draw my next breath. I also spent too many sleepless nights positive that you would give up on me, find someone else, change your mind. I could think of a million ways it was not going to work out, picture myself waiting here for hour after hour, alone."

"There's no one else, I promise," she said fervently.

He bent and pressed a kiss into that tender spot where her neck met her shoulder. "Baby, something in your voice says there's a story you're not telling me."

She blew out a hard breath and admitted, "My friends said I really had to try seeing other guys..."

He was suddenly too quiet behind her. Was he even breathing? "And did you?" he asked.

"I did, yes."

"And...?"

She winced. "You really want to hear this?"

"Damn straight I do."

She told him everything, all about her adventures in online dating, starting with the online chats and the coffee dates, moving on to the Farmer's Market day with Dave, the awful evening with the grabby podiatrist and the three dates with Ted.

When she first started putting it all out there, Matthias remained still as a statue behind her. But he slowly relaxed. He said he would like to go a few rounds with that foot doctor. And he made a sound of approval when she got to how she told Ted that she was in love with someone else and added, "Meaning you," just in case he had a single doubt by now who owned her heart.

Once she'd told him everything, she asked, "How come you didn't just come looking for me sooner? You could have saved me from all those bad dates, saved yourself from worrying that I wouldn't show up here for Christmas. I don't think I would have been that hard to find."

His hand stroked slowly along her arm, fingers brushing up and down. "That wasn't our agreement."

She slithered around again, getting front to front. "I can't believe you know that, that you understand that."

He looked vaguely puzzled. "*Should* I have tracked you down?"

"I have no idea." Sending water splashing, she rose up to kiss him and then settled back down against his broad chest. "What I do know," she said, "is that I've always felt that trying to find you between Christmases would be wrong. I felt it was important that we both respected the agreement we'd made together, that if the terms were going to change, they had to change at Christmastime."

He caught her face between his wet hands and pulled her up so her parted lips were only an inch from his. "Everything is changed, as of now. We're agreed on that, right?"

She bobbed her head up and down in his hold. "Yes, we are. I'm in. You're in. Both of us. A hundred percent."

"We're together now. We're taking this thing we have public and we're doing that before New Year's."

"Yes. You and me, in front of the whole world—have you got vacation time this year?"

His lips brushed hers again. "I'm off until January second."

"Good. We'll visit your family in Valentine Bay. I'm taking you to the farm—and we have to go to Portland. I need you to meet my best friends, Peyton and Iris."

He smiled against her mouth. "So then, we have a plan."

"Oh, yes we do."

"Make no mistake." He kissed her, hard and quick. "Marriage. We're doing it, the whole thing. The ring. The white dress. The vows— and what about kids? You do want kids?"

"Oh, Matthias. Yes. Definitely. All of the above. I can't wait to marry you."

"I think we've both waited more than long enough." But then he frowned. "Have I blown this? I should be on my knees now, shouldn't I?"

That time, *she* kissed *him*. "Naked in the bathtub is working just fine."

"All right, then." He pulled her closer and

sprinkled kisses in a line along her cheek. When he reached her ear, he whispered, "We're not just each other's Christmas present anymore. What we have is for the whole year round."

"For the rest of our lives," she vowed.

And they sealed their promise of forever with a long, sweet kiss.

Epilogue

They stayed at the cabin for Christmas, enjoying all the traditions they'd created together in the years before.

On Christmas morning, he handed her a small package wrapped in shiny red paper and tied with a white satin bow. She opened it carefully, feeling strangely expectant, full of nerves and happiness.

Inside was a ring-sized box with a porcupine carved in the top. "You made this."

"Guilty," he said in that gruff, low voice that she loved more than anything—well, except for everything else about him. She loved all that, too.

She glanced up at him. He was kind of blurry. But that happens when a girl's eyes are filled with sudden tears. "Matthias. I love you."

He reached out a hand and eased his warm, rough fingers under her hair. Clasping her nape, he pulled her in close. "Don't cry." He kissed her forehead. "It's a present. Presents shouldn't make you cry."

"Of course they should." She sniffled. "But only if they're really good ones." A couple of tears got away from her and trickled down her cheeks.

He kissed those tears, first on one cheek and then the other. Then he went for her lips. That kiss lasted a while. They were always doing that, kissing and forgetting about everything else.

Finally, Zoya gave a hopeful whine. They both glanced down to see the dog sitting at their feet, her vivid blue eyes tracking—Matthias to Sabra and back to Matthias again.

"Aww. Zoya needs love, too." With a chuckle, Sabra dropped to a crouch to give the dog a quick hug.

When she got up again, she held up the box and admired his workmanship. "It's beautiful." It even had two tiny brass hinges to keep the lid attached.

He gazed at her so steadily, a bemused expression on that face she knew she would never tire of looking at. From the speaker on the kitchen table, Mariah Carey sang "All I Want for Christmas Is You." Happiness crowded out every other emotion. She glanced away and swiped at more joyful tears.

"Sabra."

She met his eyes again. "Hmm?"

"Are you ever going to open it?"

A lovely, warm shiver went through her as she lifted the carved lid.

Inside, on a bed of dark blue velvet, a single pear-shaped diamond glittered at her from a platinum band. "Oh, you gorgeous thing," she said, the words more breath than sound.

"It's okay?" he asked, adorably anxious.

"It is exactly right. Just beyond beautiful, Matthias. Thank you." She went up on tiptoe for another quick kiss. And then she passed the open box to him. "Put it on for me?"

He did as she asked, bending to set the box on the coffee table and then sinking lower, all the way to one knee. "Sabra Bond." He reached for her left hand.

She gave it, loving the feel of his fingers

closing around hers, protective. Arousing. Companionable, too.

"I never expected you." His eyes gleamed up at her, teasing her, loving her. "You broke into my cabin and ran off with my heart." She gave a little squeak of delight at his words and brought her right hand to her own heart. "It hasn't been easy for us," he said. "We've both been messed up and messed over. And it's taken way too long for each of us to be ready at the same time. But now, here we are, four years from that first year. Finally making it work. And it all feels just right, somehow." He slipped the ring onto her finger. It did feel right, a perfect fit. "There is no one but you, Sabra. You are in my dreams at night and the one I want to find beside me when I wake up in the morning. I love you," he said. "Will you marry me?"

Those pesky, joyful tears were blurring her

vision again. She blinked them away. "Oh, yes, I will marry you, Matthias Bravo—and didn't I say that two days ago, in the tub?"

He looked at her like he might eat her right up. "No man ever gets tired of hearing the word *yes.*"

The next morning, as they were packing for their round-trip tour of farm, friends and family, Matt heard a vehicle drive into the yard.

He looked out the front window. "Terrific," he muttered, meaning it wasn't.

Sabra, descending the stairs with her suitcase in hand, laughed. "Oh, come on. It can't be that bad."

"It's Jerry," he grumbled. "He's here to check on us." Outside, his lifelong friend got out of his patrol pickup and hitched up his belt.

Sabra set the suitcase down at the base of the stairs. "Invite him in. We'll have coffee."

Jerry, mounting the porch steps, spotted Matt in the window and grinned. Matt scowled back at him.

Did a dirty look slow Jerry down? Not a chance. He kept coming, straight to the door.

Matt pulled it open. "What a surprise," he said flatly, because it wasn't. Jerry showing up with no warning was just par for the course. "Got a problem with your phone again?"

Jerry took off his hat. "You could have dropped me a text, man." He looked hurt. "Let me know that everything was working out. I kinda got worried. I just wanted to check in, make sure that you're all right."

Now Matt felt like the thoughtless one. Probably because Jerry had a valid point. "Okay. I apologize for not keeping you in the loop."

Jerry brightened instantly. "Thanks. And Merry Christmas."

Sabra, busy at the coffee maker, called, "Hi, Jerry. Coffee?"

That big, toothy smile took over Jerry's handsome face. "Sabra. Good to see you again. Coffee would be great."

Matt stepped aside and his friend came in.

Sabra served the coffee and offered some cranberry-orange bread to go with it. They sat at the table.

Jerry saw the ring and got up, grabbed Matt in a bear hug and clapped him on the back. "You lucky sonofagun. Finally, huh?" He turned to Sabra as he hitched a thumb in Matt's direction. "This guy. He's been waiting years for you."

Sabra just smiled her sweetest smile. "We've both waited. It's felt like forever. But now, at last, it's all worked out."

Jerry dropped back into his chair, ate a hunk of cranberry bread, and glanced around the cabin at the boxes on the counter and the suit-case by the stairs. "Where're you guys going?"

"All the places we didn't go in other years," Matt replied, knowing he was being need-lessly mysterious—but doing it anyway be-cause sometimes he enjoyed giving his friend a little grief.

Sabra sent him a reproachful glance and laid out their itinerary. "I have a farm in Astoria. We're going there for a couple of days, then down to Portland so I can introduce my hunky fiancé to my closest friends. And then on to Valentine Bay where I get to meet the Bravos."

"We would have been in touch when we got to town," said Matt. "I'm figuring we'll be having some kind of get-together, prob-ably at Daniel and Keely's." Back at the end of July, Daniel had married Lillie's cousin, Keely Ostergard, who had made the perennially grouchy Daniel the happiest guy alive—scratch that. *Second* happiest.

Now that he and Sabra were finally together and staying that way, Matt knew *he* was the happiest.

Jerry asked hopefully, "So are you saying I'm included for the party at Daniel's?"

"It's a promise," said Matt.

"What a great house," Matthias said when Sabra led him and Zoya up the front steps of the farmhouse.

"My great-great-grandfather built it," she informed him with pride.

She took him inside and showed him the rooms. He admired her new kitchen and agreed to start moving in right away, as soon as they were done with their holiday travels.

They left Zoya downstairs and Sabra took him up to see the second floor. She pulled him from one room to the next, saving the master suite for last.

She'd repainted it a soft blue-gray and changed out all the furniture. The new bed was king-size.

Of course, they had to try it out.

Matthias said it was a great bed. "But it could be a fold-up cot, as long as it has you in it."

An hour or so later, they put their clothes back on and went downstairs. Matthias got Zoya's leash and the three of them went out for a tour of Berry Bog Farm.

That night, Marjorie had them over for dinner. The Wilsons were so sweet, both of them beaming from ear to ear to learn that Sabra was engaged to her "young man," as they called Matthias. They were so pleased to learn that Matthias would be moving in with her at the farm.

* * *

In Portland, Sabra's friend Peyton welcomed Matt warmly. But he didn't miss the narrow-eyed looks Iris kept sending him.

They stayed in Iris's extra bedroom, which had become vacant when Peyton moved in with her longtime boyfriend a few months before. The plan was for two nights in Portland and then on to Valentine Bay.

The first night went well, Matt thought. They all got together at Peyton's. Matt liked her boyfriend, Nick. Peyton was a really good cook, so the food was terrific. They stayed late, till almost two.

In the morning, when he woke up in Iris's spare room, Sabra was still sleeping. He lay there beside her, watching her breathe, thinking that he'd never been this happy, loving the way her hair was all matted on one side of her head and admiring the thick, inky shine to her eyelashes, fanned out so prettily against the velvety curve of her cheek.

About then, as he was getting really hopelessly sappy and sentimental over this amazing woman who had actually said yes to forever with him, Zoya, over on the thick rug by the window, sat up with a whine.

She needed to go out.

He managed to get dressed, get his coat and the leash, and usher the dog out of the room without disturbing the sleeping woman in the bed.

At the door to the outer hall, he grabbed the key that Iris kept in a bowl on the entry table. Outside, it was snowing, a light, wet snow, the kind that doesn't stick. He walked the dog to the little park down the street, where they had a big playset for kids and a tube mounted on a pole containing plastic bags for dog owners who hadn't thought to bring their own.

Zoya took care of business. He cleaned up after her and then walked her through the gently falling snow. They circled the block, pausing at every tree and rock and hydrant that happened to catch the husky's eye.

Back at the apartment, he let himself in, took Zoya off her leash and followed her to the kitchen where his nose told him there was coffee.

Iris was already up, sitting at the table sipping from a mug with Me? Sarcastic? Never. printed on the side. She didn't waste any time. "We need to talk. Before Sabra gets up. It won't take long."

Iris allowed him to get out of his coat, wash his hands and pour himself some coffee. When he slid into the chair across from her, she said, "This better be for real for you, that's all I'm saying."

The thing was, he understood her concern.

Not because he was ever backing out on what he finally had with Sabra, but because of how long it had taken them to get here—and also the thing with Mary. That never should have happened. He would always feel like crap about that.

"I don't know how to say it, Iris. I love her. She's the happiness I never thought I'd find. I screwed up last year. I know that. But that was because of…" Anything he said was just going to sound like an excuse—worse. It would *be* an excuse. For his failure of belief when everything seemed hopeless, his failure to hold steady against all the odds.

Iris scoffed, "You got nothin'. Am I right?"

What could he say? "You *are* right. I should have done better. I took her at her word when she told me there was no future for us."

Iris glanced away. When she faced him again, she took a big gulp of coffee and set the cup down, wrapping her lean, dark hands around it, holding on tight.

He tried again, "The thing is, it *worked* for us, you know? The way it's all turned out, it was…right. It was what we both needed. Every step was important to find our way to this life we're going to make together from now on."

"You know that you sound just like her, right?"

"If I do, it's because she and I understand each other. You think *I* was happy when she told me that you and Peyton insisted she go out with other guys—and that she *did*?"

"She told you about that?"

"Yeah. She told me and, no, I don't like any other guy even having a prayer with her. But I get it. I get why you pushed her to do it. And I accept that it turned out to be something she *needed* to do."

Iris rose, refilled her mug and topped his off.

When she sat back down, neither of them said anything for several minutes. They sipped coffee as Zoya crunched kibble from the bowl Iris had put at the end of the counter for her.

Finally, Iris looked directly at him. "Okay, here's the deal, Matthias. I really didn't want to like you. But I kind of think I do."

In Valentine Bay, they stayed at Matthias's small house, which was perched on a hill over-looking his hometown. Now that he was moving to the farm, he would be subletting the place until the lease ran out.

Sabra liked his little house. It had two bedrooms and a small yard. In his room, he led her to his closet and shoved back a rod full of clothes to point out the calendar hanging there, every day marked with a big red X through the twenty-second of December.

"Note the large red circle around the twenty-third to the thirty-first," he said.

She grabbed him and kissed him, a long kiss full of love and wonder, just because he was hers.

When she finally let go of him, he explained, "I kept one every year from our first year—except last year," he admitted. "Last year, I bought the calendar, but then, well…"

"Come here." She pulled him close again. "I get it and there is no need to explain."

That called for another kiss, which called for another after that…

The house Matthias had been raised in wasn't far from his place. His brother Daniel and his family lived there now and also his youngest sister, Grace.

On December thirtieth, Sabra and Grace were together in the kitchen making sandwiches for lunch.

Grace mentioned Mary. Matthias's sister said that he'd brought Mary to the family Thanksgiving the year before.

"Mary's a nice woman," Grace said. "But we all knew she wasn't the one." She spread mustard on a slice of rye. "You, on the other hand…" She pointed the table knife at Sabra and fake threatened, "Don't you ever leave him."

Sabra had a one-word reply for that. "Never."

"Good answer." Grace dipped the knife in the mustard jar again and grabbed a second slice of bread. "So, have you set a date yet?"

"Not yet, but the sooner the better as far as I'm concerned."

"You want a big wedding?"

"No. Small. And simple. Just close friends and family."

"How about New Year's Day?" Grace slid her a sideways glance.

"*This* New Year's? The day after tomorrow?"

"Hey. It was just a thought…" Grace stuck the knife back in the mustard jar.

Sabra unwrapped a block of Tillamook cheddar. "I do like the way you think."

"Why, thank you." Grace held up a hand across the kitchen island and Sabra high-fived it.

"I would need to check with Matthias…"

Grace gave a goofy snort accompanied by an eye roll. "As if we don't already know what his answer's gonna be."

"…and then I would have to get on it immediately, see if my friends in Portland and at the farm might be able to swing it. And then, if they can, head for the courthouse in Astoria to get the license right away—and what about a waiting period? Isn't there one of those?"

"As a rule it's three days, but you can get the waiting period waived for a fee. I know because Aislinn got married this past year. She and her husband Jaxon went straight from the marriage license bureau to the church."

"Perfect—and what about a dress? Omigod. I need the dress!"

"Well, then, what are you waiting for? Get with Matt and then get on the phone."

They stared at each other over the half-made sandwiches. Sabra broke the silence. "I believe I will do that."

Grace let out a shout of pure glee and grabbed her in a hug.

On New Year's Day, Matt married the only woman for him. The ceremony took place in the family room right there at the house where he'd grown up.

Iris and Peyton served as maids of honor. Nils Wilson gave Sabra away. Jerry stood up as Matt's best man. Daniel's two-year-old daughter, Frannie, was the flower girl and Jake, Frannie's twin, the ring bearer. Both

Zoya and Daniel's basset hound Maisey Fae had festive collars decorated with red velvet poinsettias. Matt wore his best suit. Sabra looked more beautiful than ever in a day-length, cream-colored silk dress with a short veil.

They said their vows before the big window that looked out on the wide front porch, a cozy fire in the giant fireplace. The family Christmas tree, resplendent with a thousand twinkling lights, loomed majestic across the room as snow drifted down outside.

"Always," he promised.

"Forever," she vowed.

Matt pulled her into his arms and kissed her—that special kiss, the kiss like no other, the one that marked the beginning of their new life together as husband and wife.

* * * * *

LET'S TALK

Romance

For exclusive extracts, competitions
and special offers, find us online:

 facebook.com/millsandboon

 @millsandboonuk

 @millsandboon

Or get in touch on 0844 844 1351*

For all the latest titles coming soon,
visit millsandboon.co.uk/nextmonth